MISSING MIKE

MISSING MIKE

MIKE

by SHARI GREEN

pajamapress

www.pajamapress.ca   info@pajamapress.ca

 Canada Council Conseil des arts
for the Arts du Canada

 ONTARIO ARTS COUNCIL
CONSEIL DES ARTS DE L'ONTARIO
an Ontario government agency
un organisme du gouvernement de l'Ontario

 Canadä

The publisher gratefully acknowledges the support of the Canada Council for the Arts and the Ontario Arts
Council for its publishing program. We acknowledge the financial support of the Government of Canada
through the Canada Book Fund (CBF) for our publishing activities.

Library and Archives Canada Cataloguing in Publication

Green, Shari, 1963-, author
    Missing Mike / by Shari Green.

ISBN 978-1-77278-045-1 (hardcover)

    I. Title.

PS8613.R4283M57 2018   jC813'.6   C2018-900550-5

Publisher Cataloging-in-Publication Data (U.S.)

Names: Green, Shari, 1963-, author.
Title: Missing Mike / by Shari Green.
Description: Toronto, Ontario Canada : Pajama Press, 2018. | Summary: "Eleven-year-old Cara Donovan and
    her family flee a wildfire bearing down on their hometown of Pine Grove, with no time to find Cara's
    beloved dog Mike. Faced with the loss of everything she knows, Cara can't stand to lose Mike as well
    and seeks a way to sneak back home. When her plans are thwarted, she must learn to embrace a new
    definition of 'home'"— Provided by publisher.
Identifiers: ISBN 978-1-77278-045-1 (hardcover)
Subjects: LCSH: Dogs – Juvenile fiction. | Wildfires – Juvenile fiction. | Pet loss – Juvenile fiction. | Stories in
    rhyme. | BISAC: JUVENILE FICTION / Animals / Dogs. | JUVENILE FICTION / Nature & the Natural
    World / Disasters.
Classification: LCC PZ7.G744Mi |DDC [Fic] – dc23

Cover design—Rebecca Buchanan
Interior design and typesetting—Rebecca Buchanan, and Martin Gould / martingould.com

Manufactured by Friesens
Printed in Canada

Pajama Press Inc.
181 Carlaw Ave., Suite 207, Toronto, Ontario Canada, M4M 2S1

Distributed in Canada by UTP Distribution
5201 Dufferin Street, Toronto, Ontario Canada, M3H 5T8

Distributed in the U.S. by Ingram Publisher Services
1 Ingram Blvd., La Vergne, TN 37086, USA

for Tom

Too Close

It hasn't rained for thirty-seven days.
The air crackles in the heat
gold grass crunches
beneath my tires.
As I whip along the forest trail
climbing toward the viewpoint
Mike lopes beside my bike
barking at crickets or squirrels
or maybe for the sheer joy of it.
Heather's been away
almost three weeks
visiting her relatives.
She's due back in a day or two
but until then
it's just me and Mike.
Even though I kind of miss
hanging out with Heather
Mike
and my bike
make for a pretty great summer.

Mike's named after Mike Wazowski
the one-eyed monster
in a kids' movie

because before we got him
he lost an eye in a fight
—a bit of an ear too.
It was probably coyotes.

Now, Mike gets too close.
I swerve
and a branch whips my leg.
I stop to assess the damage
—not to my shin
where a drop of blood
already beads on the deep scratch
but to the shiny red paint
of my new mountain bike.
The bike was a birthday present
from Mom and Dad
given when school let out in June
even though I don't turn eleven
until next week.

The paint
is still perfect.
"Not a mark," I tell Mike.
I gulp down some water
pour more into my hand for Mike
then look down across the town
before glancing at the sky
—brilliant blue
marred by a thick plume of smoke
in the distance.

The wildfires are bad this year
new ones popping up every day
because of lightning
or careless people
or sparks from work vehicles
in the tinder-dry woods.
It's hard to tell
how far away the smoke is
but the tightness in my gut
says it's not far enough.

Just in Case

The entire town of Pine Grove
is on evacuation alert.
Another town north of us
was on alert for two weeks
until yesterday
when they were ordered to go.

"It doesn't mean we'll have to leave," Mom says.
"Just that we need to be ready.
If the winds change..."

She shakes her head
doesn't finish her sentence
but I've seen the news.
If the winds change
the fire alters course.
If the winds change
it could come straight for us.

warning of danger (5 letters)
A L E R T

Mom wears a frown set firmly
beneath worried eyes

as she hurries around the house
collecting treasures
and necessities
packing them into plastic bins.
I'm not always clear
on which things are treasures
and which are necessities
but I don't question her.

"Girls," she says to me and Sloane,
"I need you to put the earthquake kit
in the car
then pack an overnight bag."

Our earthquake kit is two blue bins
stacked one on the other
in the corner of our laundry room.
Mom stocked those bins last year
after reading about earthquakes
and how important it was
to be ready.
I don't think we really get earthquakes here
but at least we'll have supplies
if it ever happens.

Sloane and I lug the bins outside
load them
into the trunk of Mom's car.
Mike Wazowski follows us out
nuzzles my bare leg
with his wet nose.

I scratch his rust-colored back
and he promptly flops down on the driveway
rolls over
so I can rub his belly too.

When Mike and I head to the backyard
and start up a game of fetch
Mom calls me back inside.
She marches me to my room
so I can't get distracted
again.

The overnight bag.
Right.

My school backpack rests in a corner
crammed with papers, artwork, markers
even though school let out
over a month ago.
Mom yanks open the zipper
dumps the contents on my bed
shakes out pencil shavings
and a shower of paper clips.

"A change of clothes
and a few treasures," she says.

I pick up the stack of crossword books
on my nightstand
open the maw of my pack
to stuff them in.

"No," Mom says. "Important things
—things you can't live without.
Just in case."

The *just in case* lands in my stomach
like a glowing coal
burns a hole
in my gut.
Just in case
means the unimaginable.

I'd give anything
to stop imagining it.

Important Things

Two crossword books
because if I only take one
and I finish all its puzzles
what will I do
when there's nothing
to do?

Pencils
with good erasers
and a sharpener.

Mike's leash
—the spare one.
And his favorite toy
with the squeaker
that drives Mom mad.

Shorts
t-shirt
underwear
pajamas
—the purple ones
that aren't too warm
for summer.

Flopsy Rabbit
because even though I'm almost eleven
and shouldn't need
to sleep with Flopsy
I suspect *she* might need
to sleep with me.
She's not particularly brave
for a stuffed bunny.

I tuck Flopsy's ears down
so they don't get zipped
in the zipper
close my pack
set it on the floor
at the foot of my bed
ready
just in case.

Go!

I kneel on the prickly grass in the backyard
brushing Mike Wazowski.
Fluffy clumps of his hair
blow across the yellow lawn
cartwheeling like tumbleweeds
in the desert.
Poor dog. I can't imagine
wearing a fur coat in this heat.
Mike inches away
as if he'd like nothing better
than to take off
in search of shade
or adventure
or both, if he's lucky.

"Come on back here, you."
Talking to Mike makes me cough.
The air stinks
like old campfire ashes
and breathing it in
day after day
has pestered my throat.

I peer over our busted-up fence
to the hills outside of town.
Dark gray smoke mounds up
tumbles over itself
clambers for a higher and higher perch.
It's close—too close.
No wonder Mike's skittish.
I rub him behind his ears
then turn my attention back
to his excess fur
thinking I'll get the hose when I'm done
cool us both off.

Mom's voice cuts through the air
sharp and strange.
"Cara!
Inside—now."

With another glance
at the sky
I know what she's really saying:
danger
evacuation
time to go.

I drop Mike's brush
tell him to stay—"I'll be right back"
—dash inside
discover Mom
throwing canned goods into a laundry basket

and a police officer
standing in the front doorway.

Ten minutes.
Ten minutes to pack up and leave our home.
Ten minutes to grab our just-in-case backpacks
and as much food and clothing
as we can
toss it all into the trunk
with the emergency bins
full of bottled water
protein bars and a baggie of Mike's kibble
first-aid kit, radio, flashlight, tarp
and matches—which is about the stupidest thing
ever.

All Mom's ready-for-anything planning
seems completely useless now
ready for nothing
because how could you ever be ready
to run for your lives?

Dad's pickup squeals into the driveway.
He leaps out
still wearing dirty coveralls from work
forgets to slam the truck door
gathers me up in a too-hard hug.
He smells of motor oil and sweat.

"Where's your mother? Where's Sloane?"

"They're coming," I say.
"Just getting more stuff."

He releases me
tells me to grab Mike and get in the car
then disappears into the house
hollering Mom's name.

I unlatch the gate
slip through and go around back
for Mike
find his brush where I abandoned it
on the lawn.
I whistle
call Mike's name
cough
and call again.
Smoke stings my eyes.

Mike's not in the yard
probably jumped clear over the lousy fence
searching for a cool spot
a not-so-smoky spot
a safe spot.
The creek—that's where he'd go.
He doesn't know it's dried up
a river of dust and twigs and stones
not a drop of clear cool water
for miles.

I dash around the house to the front
planning to grab my bike
and head for the road.
It'll be quicker
than hopping fences in back.

Dad's arm shoots out
stops me
steers me
toward the car.
"Where's Mike?" he asks
and I tell him Mike's gone
and I have to find him—I know
I can find him.
I just need time.

"There's no time," Dad says.

Of course there's time
—we can't go without him.
I pull away from Dad
but he moves with me, blocking me.
"We have to go," Dad says.

"We can't leave him!"

I twist away
run for my bike
yank it from where it leans
against the front porch
and hop on.

Dad grabs the handlebars.

I shout at him
—"Let go!
I have to find Mike!"
and I wrench the handlebars
one way
the other
give up and leap
from the bike.
Dad catches me around the waist
and my bike clatters
to the ground
arms and legs flail
as I try to escape.
"Mike!"

From the porch
Mom commands: "Cara.
Get in the car
now."

Something in her voice
takes the fight right out of me.
Dad loosens his hold
sets me down.
I lift my gaze
look beyond the car, the yard, the town
to the dry hills.
It's not just smoke
from somewhere beyond.

The fire's close—flames raging
shooting bright orange into the sky
consuming the pine forest.
The heat wallops me
makes me step back
even though I'm way over here
in Pine Grove
way over here
across hills, highway, neighborhood, yard.
I can't say a word.
I climb into the car with my parents
my sister
my just-in-case backpack
and we go.

The Road Out

Dad backs onto the road
all of us strapped in
amidst the clutter of spare shoes
photo albums
Nana's handmade quilts
our eyes streaming
from smoke or sadness
or both.
We start driving away
but we're only in front of our neighbor's house
when Mom says, "Wait!"
I snap to attention
—*Mike?*

But no.
Mom opens her door
gets out
raises her phone to take a picture
of our home
as if she's already given up hope
it'll be here
when we get back.
I sag
against the seat.

After the grabbing, packing, running
cramming things
into our car
I expect us to race down the streets
hit the highway at top speed
as we flee.
But the route's clogged with cars
everyone evacuating at the same time
one road
leading to safety.

"I could've found him
by now.
I could've found him
and caught up with you."

I beg Dad to please, please go back
but even as the words escape
I'm half terrified he'll do it
turn us right around
aim us toward the flames
and that wall
of heat.

"I'm sorry," he says
and I can tell
he means it.
"It's too dangerous."

As we inch along
I crane my neck to peer out one window

then another
hoping for a glimpse of rusty fur
wagging tail
but the minutes tick by
with no sign
of Mike.

It's dim
ash and smoke choking out the light
of the mid-afternoon sun.
Ahead of us, a string of taillights stretches out
as we crawl toward the city
Dad white-knuckling the steering wheel
Mom taut and tight-lipped
and none of us
saying a word.

I look to Sloane
beside me in the backseat
hope for reassurance
some big-sister words of wisdom
telling me this whole situation
isn't as bad
as it looks.
She sits straight-backed
clutching her ukulele in its case
and gnawing
on a hangnail.
She stares wide-eyed
through the windshield.
I turn away.

Something *thunks*
on the hood of our car.
Mom shrieks
Dad brakes
seatbelt yanks hard
against my chest.
"It's nothing," Dad says. "Debris."
He starts driving again.

Beside the road, spruce and pine line up
like rows and rows of soldiers.
They stand silently
not sensing the attack
coming from behind.
Flames dart among branches
edging closer
so near the front lines.
Sparks shower down
bright orange sparklers tossed
from burning trees
onto dry grass
at the side of the highway.

"I think we're going the wrong way," I say
because this is worse than at home.
This is *more* dangerous.
We should be running away from the flames
but instead
we're heading straight for them.
Panic rises
threatens to close my throat.

"Turn around!
Dad, you have to turn around!"

Without sparing me a glance
he says, "Road's closed the other way, Cara.
This is the only way out."

My fists
and stomach
clench.

Two deer dash past the car
hurrying along the shoulder of the road
escaping faster than we are.
My heart races
to catch up.

It feels like we've been driving for hours
but we haven't come to the city
haven't left the fire behind.
It seems to follow us
taunting with its rain of ash
hurling sparks as if to say
you can't outrun me
and for the first time I wonder
if we really can't.

Can Mike?

Dad pulls over
stops the car
opens his door and climbs out

as heat and smoky air
rush in.
I unbuckle
lean forward to see what's going on.
Mom points—another car
on the side of the road
a thin man standing beside it
shirt collar pulled up
over his nose and mouth.
A pickup truck parks behind us.
The driver strides over to Dad
and the three men talk
gesture
hesitate
then a decision's made.
The thin man opens the rear door of his car
lifts out a baby's car seat
draped with pink cloth
rushes to the truck
and gets in.
Dad and the truck's driver pull garbage bags
suitcases
a flat of bottled water
from the thin man's car trunk
toss it all in the back of the truck.
When Dad settles into his seat next to Mom
he's red-faced and sweaty.

"Ran out of gas," he says
and I see Mom peer past him
at our own gas gauge.

Darkness

It's dark as night
—black smoke so thick
I can barely see the car ahead of us.
Wind hurls glowing embers
across the road
orange sparks fly
like hailstones made of fire.
Sweat beads on my forehead.

Sudden movement
just ahead on the right
—burning tree
crashes through branches
falling
a tower of flame
cast onto the shoulder
of the road.
Dad swears under his breath.

"This is insane," Mom says.
She twists around
checks on me and Sloane
turns back to read the gas gauge
again.

If we run out of fuel
will someone stop to help us?
What happens if we're stranded
in the fire zone?
What happens
if we can't get out?

I pull my backpack onto my lap
meaning to open it
find Flopsy
or a crossword book
for distraction
for comfort
for *something*
but I can't bring myself
to unzip the pack.
I hug it to my chest
tuck my chin down
and close my eyes.

Rescue

The line of traffic spreads out
and picks up speed.
The air's still thick with ash
but the trees alongside us are green
no flames snapping in the wind
no sparks plummeting
to the ground.

I release my seatbelt, twist around
onto my knees
peer out the rear window
as we get farther and farther
from home
farther and farther
from Mike.
I imagine him on the shoulder
of the road
confused
wondering why on earth
I left him.
I imagine him running to catch up
finding us
finding *me*

but he's not there.

I blink away the not-seeing-him
lift my gaze from the road
to the sky
and for a moment
the twisted knot of worry in my belly
loosens.
It shouldn't feel beautiful, I know
but I can't stop staring
—red-ball sun
in a molten sky
and trees dark as shadows
in the smoke.
"You should look," I say to Sloane.
Sloane's arms clamp tightly across her chest
as her face turns away.

"Buckle up," Mom says.

I turn around just as Dad
hits the brakes
and I tumble forward
face smacking the back
of the driver's seat.
I crumple
fall awkwardly into the small space
knees and elbows jutting
into seat
floor
door.

"Cara!" Mom shouts, half worried
half mad.

Sloane peers down at me
eyebrows pulled together.
"You okay?" she asks.

"Fine," I say
as I haul myself
back where I should be.

Sloane's expression relaxes
then twists into a smirk.
She taps her seatbelt buckle
shakes her head.
"Dummy," she says.
Mom doesn't call her on it
probably because at this moment
Sloane's right.

Mom turns her worried-mad attention
to Dad
demands to know
why he stopped so suddenly.

"It ran out," he says, "then went back.
I'm lucky I didn't hit it."

He points out his side window
where a black-and-white cat
ears flat

crouches in the dust
directly across from me.
As quick as it takes Mom to say
"Poor thing"
my seatbelt's off again
door wide open
legs pulled up to make room.
The cat stares at me
like it's sizing me up.
Its tail twitches.

"Cara, we can't—"
Before Dad can finish his sentence
the cat bolts for the car
leaps in.
I close the door
speak softly to the cat
and put on my seatbelt.
Dad sighs
and resumes driving.

Cling

Sloane's not much of a fan of animals
which the cat
seems to find appealing.
When it finally dares to creep
from floor
to seat
it chooses Sloane's lap
to rest on.
She doesn't pet it.

"Check if it's a girl
or a boy," I say.

Her nose wrinkles
as if my words
were a nasty smell.

"Not a chance," she says.

"How am I supposed to know
what to name it?"

"It doesn't need
a name."

I tell her that of course
it needs a name
just like people
deserve proper names.
How would she like it
if everyone called her
Hey You her whole life?

She shifts her ukulele case
so it stands on its end
between her feet.
"It's just a cat," she says.

"Why are you so mean?"

"Why are you such a pain?"

Mom twists around
in her seat.
"Girls," she says. "Please.
We're all a bit tense right now—"

"You think?" says Sloane
earning herself a sharp look
from Mom.

"We're all worried," Mom says.
"We're all scared.
Give each other some grace
all right?"

"How about I give her the cat?"
Sloane says
grasping it around the belly
and lifting.
The cat has other ideas.
Its claws latch onto Sloane's shirt
cling fiercely.
Sloane disconnects one paw
goes to work on the next
but already the cat
is hooked on again.
Sloane gives up
plunks the cat
back
on her lap.

I feel a bit like the cat
like I'm an annoyance
she has to put up with
but I hang on
in the hope
she'll get back to being her old self
back to liking her little sister
again.

Needed

Two summers ago
after an entire year of pleading
I managed to convince my parents
I was ready
to own a dog.
The way I saw it
I'd been ready my whole life
but it wasn't until I turned nine
they finally said yes.

We drove to Braeburn
where there's an animal shelter.
Sloane didn't say much on the way
but I couldn't stop chattering
too excited to keep words
from flying out of me.
Sloane put in her earbuds
and pretended
I wasn't there.

Inside the shelter
a man took us to the back
to see the animals available
for adoption.

A family with three kids clamored
at a kennel door
where five fluffy goldendoodle pups
wiggled and yipped
and tried to outdo one another
in cuteness.
Mom peered around the family
*ooh*ing and *aah*ing
at the puppies
but I wandered away
to visit the other dogs.
That's when I saw Mike.
He wasn't a puppy
and he wasn't cute
but I was pretty sure
he needed somebody
to love him.

"He's a sweetheart,"
said the man who worked there.
"I'm glad his injuries
healed so well."

Mike wasn't nose-to-the-door eager
like most of the other dogs.
Instead he lay in the back corner
of his kennel
chin on his front paws
awake
but not paying any mind
to the commotion.

It was almost as if he was quite certain
he wouldn't be chosen
so why get excited?

"Cara," Mom called. "Look at these cuties.
Aren't they the sweetest things?"
I walked over as she pointed
at one of the goldendoodle pups
—a female, the worker told us.
"What about this one?" Mom said
smiling and sounding so sure
she'd found the perfect dog
for me.
It *was* adorable
I have to admit
but something pulled me back
to Mike.

I crouched at the door to his kennel
talked to him
voice quiet
so it was just between us.
"I know what it's like
being ignored," I said.
"I know what it's like
not getting picked."

His ears twitched.

"See that girl over there?"
I nodded toward Sloane

leaning against the wall
with her arms crossed.
"That's my sister.
We used to do a lot together
but lately
she mostly ignores me.
And at my school
—picking teams
in gym?
Not fun at all."

Mike sat up then
and cocked his head
peering at me out of his one eye
all curious-like
as if he was wondering whether I was someone
he might like to get to know.
"I'd sure like a chance
to get to know *you*,"
I told him.

Mom and Dad tried to convince me
to look at other dogs.
The other family had already picked
one of the male goldendoodles
and I knew
Mom still had her eye
on that female.
But would anyone want
the skinny
grown-up

already-got-in-a-fight
dog
with one eye
and a tattered ear?

Sloane spoke up. "That one
looks like he needs a good home."
Her face was turned toward me and Mike.
How long
had she been watching us?

"He'll already have bad habits,"
Mom said.

"If he's been in a fight once
he'll get in trouble again,"
Dad said.

Mike was standing then
and his tail
started wagging.

"He's saying
he won't be a problem,"
I told Mom and Dad
and right then
Mike raised one front leg
like he wanted to shake a paw.
"See? He wants to shake on it.
You can always trust a dog
who's willing
to shake your hand."

The look on Dad's face
said he wasn't so sure.

"I think we should get him,"
Sloane said.

I don't know if she could tell
Mike and I
were meant to be
or if she was just disagreeing
with Mom and Dad
because that was sort of starting to be
her thing.
But either way
when the man who worked there
raved about Mike's sweet nature
Mom and Dad finally came around
and said okay.

"I expect he had a good home once,"
he told us. "I figure he got lost
when his owners were traveling
in the area."

Dad clipped a leash to Mike's collar
as the man
gave us instructions.
"He was probably on his own
for quite some time
before he got hurt," he said.
"He's not used to being cooped up.

You'll have to watch
he doesn't run off.
You'll have to be careful
to keep him safe."

The moment Mom opened the back door
of our car
Mike jumped in
sat tall on the seat
king of the car
until Mom shooed him
onto the floor
and took off the leash.
When the car began moving
Mike stood in front of me
stepping on my toes
so he could enjoy the view
out the side
and coating my window
with nose prints.
I gave his rusty fur
a gentle scratch
where it was soft on his chest
ran my fingers over his silky ears
careful of the left one
in case it was still tender
and just then
my heart was so full
I could barely breathe.

That night I thanked Sloane
for taking my side
for helping convince Mom and Dad.

"I didn't do it for you," she said
like she wouldn't want me thinking
she was really
on my team
but I'm pretty sure
she was.

Not Home

The police officer back in Pine Grove
gave us directions
for the evacuation route
but we don't need them.
The long snake of traffic leads us through the city
and finally
slithers right into the crowded parking lot
of a community center.

Dad drives up and down rows
of cars, pickups, RVs
then pulls into a parking spot
that's not really a whole spot
but it's the best
he can find.
He shuts off the engine
and Mom lets out a long breath
massages the back of her neck.
"Finally," she says.
"It took twice as long
as that trip normally takes
but we made it."

"Three hours of hell," Dad says
rubbing his face
not even caring
that Mom doesn't like us to use
that word.

Sloane reluctantly gathers the cat
into her arms
and we climb out of the car
into the sweltering heat
sky painted a sickly yellow-gray
smell of hot pavement and dry grass
mixing with the smoke
prickling our noses
—but at least we can breathe
without coughing.

A man wearing an orange safety vest
greets us
points us toward glass double doors.
We step inside
and air-conditioned coolness
rushes to welcome us.
Because of the cat
a woman takes us down a long hallway
to a small gym that's been converted
to a kennel
crates of all sizes
lined up in rows
barks and whimpers and the soothing voices
of volunteers

comforting, feeding, visiting
with the animals.
"It's not ours," Sloane says
about the cat
and I pipe up, "We rescued it!"

deliver or save from harm (6 letters)
R E S C U E

Even though it makes no sense
that Mike would be here
that he somehow beat us
to the evacuation center
I dare to hope
anyway
because sometimes the impossible
turns out to be
possible.
I march over to one of the volunteers
ask if she's seen a sweet-natured
rust-colored
one-eyed dog.

"Sorry," she says.
"I'd remember a dog like that
for sure."

I should know better
than to hope
for the impossible.

The volunteer mentions some paperwork to Mom
says they're all out of forms
for the Animal Response Team
but we should check back
later.
What good is *later*
when Mike is missing *now?*

The black-and-white cat
is given a temporary home
—a small plastic crate
with a wire door.
I can already tell
the cat hates it.

The woman who led us to the kennel room
takes us back the way we came
ushers us into a much larger gym
probably big enough
for floor hockey, badminton, basketball
all happening at the same time.
The room hums with activity
so many strangers
a mix of vest-clad volunteers
weary travelers
wide-eyed kids clinging to their parents' hands.
Rows and rows of cots
fill much of the floor space
piles of belongings
tucked beneath the makeshift beds
and I remember

it wasn't only Pine Grove
driven out by the fire
not only friends and neighbors
desperate for somewhere safe.

A truth zooms through me
squeezes my insides
settles
heavy as a brick:
this place
these strangers
this makeshift home that is anything
but home...
we're meant to stay here.

Kind Strangers

Dad registers us
leaves our names
birthdates
our address in Pine Grove.
While I wait
my shirt grows damp with sweat
under my backpack
so I swing the pack down
onto one arm
nearly thump a stroller
rolling by
pushed by a mom
with two more kids trailing behind her.
I look around for the thin man
and his baby girl
but don't see them.

A woman passes bottles of water
to us.
"You must be hungry,"
she says to Mom
with a nod at me and Sloane.
"I'm afraid you've missed dinner
but there are tables at the back." She points.

"Sandwiches. Coffee. Juice.
Help yourselves."

We pick our way through the maze
of people and cots
find ham sandwiches and oatmeal cookies.
Dad catches up to us
pours himself coffee
from an enormous silver urn.

"They're pretty much full," he says to Mom
with a glance across the packed gymnasium.
"They're making other arrangements
for us."

Wait—we're *not* staying?

We nibble and wonder and worry.
"Do you think Heather's here?" I ask.
"She was supposed to get home
from her trip today."

Dad passes Mom his coffee
lifts me up
for a better view.
I scan the room slowly
but there's no sign
of Heather or her family.

Sloane glances around half-heartedly
like she doesn't really expect to find

anyone she's looking for.
Most of her friends are from Braeburn
so she only sees them
at school.
Braeburn hasn't been evacuated
—not yet, at least
so of course
her friends aren't here.

Dad's halfway through his second cup of coffee
by the time a plan
comes together.
Turns out, some of the people from Pine Grove
will stay here
and some will go to the hotel across the street
some will drive farther south
to stay with friends or relatives
and some—like us   will stay with host families
people in the city who've volunteered
to take us in.

We're matched with a woman
named Jasmeet Bains.
She hugs my mom
shakes hands with my dad
smiles
at me and Sloane.
She hands Dad a small map with directions.

"In case I lose you along the way,"
she says.

We go outside
climb back into the car
follow Mrs. Bains in her SUV
as she winds through city streets
turns into a neighborhood
pulls up
in front of a tidy two-story house.
I hug my just-in-case backpack to my chest
trail behind my parents
into the home
of kind strangers.

Mrs. Bains introduces us to her husband, Bill.
"The boys are at their uncle's farm
for the summer," Mrs. Bains says,
"but you'll meet Jewel
in the morning."
She offers food
but all we want now
is sleep.
A spare bedroom for my parents
a pullout couch in the family room
for Sloane and me.
"I'd put you in the boys' room," she says
"but Bill's painting in there."

Mom tries to fuss over me
asks me over and over
if I'll be okay here
sleeping next to a stranger's TV.

For once I'm like Sloane
and have no words.

I don't brush my teeth
because how was I supposed to remember
to grab my toothbrush
during our ten-minute rush?
I crawl into bed
curl on my side
with Flopsy
take care not to kick Sloane.
A night-light casts a faint glow.
I'm glad Mrs. Bains plugged it in for us
even though I'm not afraid
of the dark anymore.
It's a little kid's night-light
a sun
with a happy face
and my mind
goes to this afternoon's red sun
the sparks
the flames
the choking smoke
and Mike
left out there to find safety
on his own.
My stomach works itself into a familiar knot
twisting around
until I wish I hadn't eaten
the ham sandwich
at the community center.

Tears well up
overflow
and I press my face
into the not-mine pillow
and cry.

Stink Eye

I'm small for my age.
Puny, actually.
First day of second grade
I walked in
not sure I had the right class
couldn't see my friends.
In front of everyone
the teacher asked if I was looking
for the kindergarten room
—kindergarten!
When she figured out I belonged
she made me sit
in front.

I told Sloane at recess.
Sloane is four years older
than I am.
She's not tall either
but she acts tall.
She walked me back to my class
zapped the kids and Mrs. Blake
with her sixth-grade glare
and all the while
she held my hand.

Some kids would be embarrassed
holding hands with their sister
but not me.
Not Sloane.
Facing my class like that
while she stood beside me
and gave them all the stink-eye
made me feel
I could handle anything.

Somewhere along the line
I stopped needing her
to glare for me
and she stopped wanting to be near enough
to do it.
I've no idea
how we fit together anymore.
All I know is
I wouldn't mind
if she held my hand
right now.

Imagining

Made-up images race
through my mind
keep me awake
tell me what-if stories
about Mike.

What if...

Mike follows the cars
the way he follows my bike
up the hill
to the view point
and the shoulder of the road
becomes a trail
the taillights
of all the vehicles evacuating
turn into a beacon
showing him the way
when the smoke makes it tough
to see...

What if...

he runs

and runs
tongue lolling
chasing me like it's a game
until he's panting hard
weary
muscles aching
and he lies down beside the road
to catch his breath...

What if...

a car stops
and a girl in the backseat
opens her door
invites him in
and he knows
—he just knows she's going
where he needs to be
so he gets up
trots over and jumps into the car
thankful for the ride
and a break from the smoke
and he settles in
for the drive to the community center
half on the girl's lap
half off
the way he's always trying
to pass himself off
as a lap dog...

What if?

Words

I unzip my pack
dig around for a crossword book
and a pencil.
Sloane's still asleep
and the house is quiet.
I sit cross-legged on a thick-cushioned chair
work on a puzzle
with an animal theme.

always keeps his luggage with him (8 letters)

I groan at the bad joke
luggage
for trunk
and fill in the squares: *E L E P H A N T.*
The *L* leads to *L I Z A R D*
and then

man's best friend (3 letters)

I scoff at how easy the clue is
change it to *girl's best friend*
before filling in the answer:
D O G.

Mike really is an excellent friend
always up for exploring
and he listens
when I need to talk.
But now...
Now I don't even know where he is
or if he's okay.

A girl pokes her head into the room
gestures for me to come over.
I swallow my worries about Mike
close the puzzle book
glad for something to pull my thoughts
away.
I follow the girl upstairs
into a bedroom with lime green walls
white curtains
and a rainbow-striped quilt on the bed.
The girl—Jewel—is taller than I am
and curvier.
Everything about her is bright
—her grin
her clothes
the energetic sparkle
in her eyes.
Her skin's white
and lightly freckled
not brown
like Mr. and Mrs. Bains'.

"Are you adopted?" I ask
then right away wonder
if that's a rude question.
Jewel grins
and shakes her head.
"You, um...don't look
like your parents."
She bursts out laughing.

"Foster kid," she says.

Asking possibly-rude questions
probably isn't the best way
to start off getting to know someone
but Jewel doesn't seem to mind.
She plunks onto the bed
knees up
leaving room for me.

"What was it like?" she asks
and I'm pretty sure she means the fire
the evacuation
the fear
and I tell her a little about it
but mostly I tell her
about leaving Mike.

"You didn't *leave* him," she says.
"He got lost."

I wish that were really true
wish I hadn't been afraid
wish I'd refused to get in the car
and forced Dad to wait
so I could look for Mike.
But I didn't.
I'm like the bad guy in a movie
a brute or a bully
and it feels
horrible.
How could I do that
to Mike?

"I hate that I left him," I tell her.
"But it's the truth."

I think of my puzzle
girl's best friend
and I imagine a new clue
a new answer
for a make-believe crossword:

girl who abandons her dog (7 letters)
V I L L A I N

Jewel's voice is firm. "No," she says,
"he got lost.
It makes a big difference
what words you use
to tell something."

She's right about words
but I've no idea
what she's getting at.

"He got lost," she says again,
"which means he can get
found."

Good Idea

The day after we brought Mike home
from the shelter
he jumped the back fence
even though Dad had patched
the worst
of the broken boards.
Mom drove me all around our neighborhood
looking for him
her lips pinched shut the whole time
like she was trying hard
not to say
what I'm sure she was thinking:

I knew that dog
was a bad
idea.

Mike came home on his own
right in time for dinner.
But I still worried
Mom was right
still worried
Mike might not want to stay.

After all
he'd been finding dinner somewhere
before he ended up
at the shelter
so maybe
he didn't need me.

A few nights later
when all the windows were open
letting the finally-cool evening air
drift in through the screens
we heard them:

coyotes

yipping and howling
in the wild space
beyond our backyard.

Mike slunk
to the living room.
I found him lying in the space
between two upholstered chairs
trembling
ears pulled down flat
and I could only imagine
what was going through his mind
—memories
of being hurt
coyotes barking and biting

tearing his ear
wrecking his eye.

I lay close beside him
rested one hand on his back.
"It's okay," I whispered.
"You're safe here."
I stayed beside him
stretched out on the floor
feeling his warmth under my hand
until the howling stopped
and he finally
relaxed.

Maybe he'd always found dinner
but without a home
who'd been there
to comfort him?
Who'd been there
to give him love?
Not having enough love
is even worse
than not having enough food
if you ask me.

A week later
I heard coyotes again
when I was biking to the lookout
Mike running beside me.
I'd taken the leash off
worried it would trip us both up

and besides
there was no traffic at all
on that old road.
Mike lagged behind from time to time
stopping to play with pinecones
or dashing into the underbrush
after squirrels
who taunted him
with their squeaks and chirps.
Mike had been gone a couple minutes
when I stopped at the top
of a hill
set my bike on its side
and caught a glimpse of him
far ahead.
"How'd you get way up there?"
I called.

A second later
I knew it wasn't Mike.

The coyote barked.
I bent down slowly
reaching
for my bike.
Why was he watching me?
My skin prickled.
Go away.
Please
go
away.

The yip-howl of other coyotes
rose in the distance
and the coyote on the road
howled back.
Noise to my right
—something crashing through the woods
my heart pounding wildly
and thank goodness
it was Mike
probably trying to get away
from the howling noise
he hates so much.
But then
Mike planted himself in front of me
hackles raised
not cowering at all.
A growl rumbled
in his throat.

When the coyote finally
trotted off the road
disappeared into the forest
I sank down beside my bike
in the dust
wrapped my arms
around Mike's neck
and held tight.
He was trembling.

I think
I was too.

"You're a brave dog
Mike Wazowski."

He licked my face
and I laughed
wiping away his slobber
with my sleeve.
"I love you too,"
I told him.

Hope

Jewel is thirteen
so maybe she knows more than I do
but there's no way
she can know for sure
Mike will be found
no way she knows
if he discovered a safe spot
where he could keep cool
and breathe
or if someone stopped their car
opened their door to let him jump in
like a certain black-and-white cat.
But
I have to believe she's right
because not believing
hurts.

A lot.

"We'll make posters," Jewel says.
"You have a picture?"

I shake my head.

Why don't I have a picture
of *girl's best friend?*
Because my best friend
was almost always with me
that's why.
I didn't need a photo
could look at his Wazowski face
any old time
I pleased.
If I'd ever imagined
he would be left behind one day
I'd have taken a thousand pictures
or maybe
a million.

Jewel gnaws her lip, thinking.
"Does he have any special markings?
Anything to help describe him?"

I laugh
a surge of joy
thankful for the first time
for what Mike went through
before I got him.
I tell her Mike's missing his left eye
and a chunk
of his left ear flap.

"So he's ugly?" she says.

"No! He's a survivor." I say it
without thinking
but it gives me hope.

We set to work designing posters
on the Bains' computer.
Turns out, Mom does have a picture
of me and Mike
on her phone
so we upload it
add it to the poster
type Mom's cell number at the bottom
and click Print.

"Mike can't be the only animal
that's missing," Jewel says
as the printer churns out page
after page.

Of course he's not.
The thought makes me feel both better
and worse.

I tell Jewel about the pet shelter
at the evacuation center
—how some of the animals
came with their owners
but others
like the black-and-white cat
were lost
and then found.

There's got to be a plan
to connect animals with their owners.
"There's supposed to be a form,"
I say, "and I bet
there's a website."
Jewel's practically a pro
at the computer
finds a site in no time
and posts Mike's picture.
If someone finds him
they can say so right there
under his sweet
survivor
face.

Mrs. Bains grabs her purse and keys.
She's off to the community center
volunteering
at the registration desk
for more evacuees.
"Is another family going to stay here?" I ask.
I imagine more kids
squeezing into the TV room
with me and Sloane
strangers added
to an already strange situation.

"I doubt that'll be necessary," she says.
"There are plenty
of volunteer hosts.

Practically the whole city's helping out
one way or another."

She invites Jewel and me to come along
bring one of our posters
check the pet shelter again
just in case.
Mom says okay
and I'm ready
in a jiffy.

The same volunteer I talked to
when we brought in the cat
crouches
in front of a large crate.
When she sees us
coming toward her
she tucks a dog treat
through the door of the crate
straightens up and dusts off her hands.

"I'm Cara," I say
my stomach suddenly fluttery.
"And this is Jewel."

"Rose Schreiber," she says.
"What can I do for you girls?"

I ask if anyone's heard news
of a one-eyed dog.

"Ah," she says. "I remember.
You were here last night
dropping off a cat."
She shakes her head.
"Sorry. Not yet."

She indicates a bulletin board
where I can tack up a poster
tells me they've got more forms now
and I should take one
from the pile on the table
fill it out
bring it back.
"Might help," she says
bending over
and opening the wire door
of a large crate.
A black lab sticks its head out
and Rose snaps a leash
onto its collar.
"Now if you'll excuse me," she says,
"I've got to take this sweetheart
for a walk.
Good luck."

Jewel pins up the poster
while I grab a form
—a complicated
fill-in-all-these-boxes form
that reads
like a tricky crossword puzzle.

Jewel peers over my shoulder
and grimaces.
She says, "Maybe
we should just call the S.P.C.A.
when we get back to the house."

"I can figure this out," I say.
"But let's call anyway
in case they've already found him."

After tracking down the black-and-white cat
giving it a good scratch
behind the ears
gentle rub
on its cheek
I take a last long look
at the faces peeking out
from Mike-sized crates
and worry gobbles up
the starting-a-search hope
inside me.

Connection

Mrs. Bains speaks with the Volunteer Coordinator
and quick as a tail wag
Jewel and I are put to work.
The big room in the community center
seems different after sleep and food
and a little time.
Was it really only yesterday we were here
not knowing what to do
where to go
where we'd stay?
This morning the clutter of belongings
looks less like chaos
and more like a collection
of saved things.
But when Jewel and I wander around
handing out gift bags
of toothbrushes, toothpaste, mini shampoos
and pointing out places
to charge phones
I see on people's faces
that they feel the same as I do
—glad to be safe
but wishing more than anything
they could go back home. .

A woman with short gray hair
and a tanned, deeply-lined face
accepts a gift bag
thanks me
says, "This is perfect.
I never thought
to bring my toothbrush."
I laugh
tell her, "Me neither."
I should carry on with my job
catch up to Jewel
but instead
I set down the rest of the bags
perch on the edge
of the woman's cot
ask if she's from Pine Grove too.
"No," she says. "I have a ranch
an hour or so northeast of there.
My son's still in the fire zone
getting the last of the animals
to safety."

Her eyes water.
I want to tell her about Mike
but I suspect she has enough worries
of her own.
"I hope they're all okay," I say.

She reaches for my hand
gives it a little pat.

"Thank you," she says.
"I hope so too."

I gather up the extra gift bags
hesitate
before walking away.
Even though she's a stranger
she feels like an ally
like a friend I didn't know I had.
Maybe all we have in common
is the need for a toothbrush
and a love
for animals
or maybe
there's more.
She knows what it's like
to leave
to run
to be away from home
and full of worry
and I bet
she's as surprised as I am
that a terrible happening
can make strangers
feel like kin.

Comfort

I stay up late
working on a puzzle
until Sloane's ready for bed.
She flicks the light off.
The night-light responds
with a faint glow
and a hint of light creeps in
along the edge of the window blinds
from the streetlamp outside.
But until my eyes adjust
I can see only shapes
—the upholstered chair
the television cabinet
the lump that is Sloane
beneath the covers.

I used to be afraid of the dark
until I got Mike.
After he settled in
at our house
he and I found a routine:
every night
when I clicked off the lamp

Mike would curl up on the mat
beside my bed.
Mom would peek in
say goodnight
ease the door closed
and the slice of light from the hallway
would be swallowed up
by the night.
I'd shift over in bed
pat the mattress
and a moment later Mike would jump
onto my bed
circle three times
create the comfiest spot
then flop down next to me
—or sometimes
half on top of me.

I was never scared
with him beside me
not even on the darkest
of dark winter nights.

Maybe it was only about his own comfort
about claiming a soft spot
to sleep
(but knowing to wait
until Mom closed the door
so she wouldn't shoo him
off the bed)

but I like to think
he knew
I needed him beside me
the moment the light
disappeared.

Streetlamps and night-lights
and even an older sister
sharing the bed
don't come close
to matching the comfort
of Mike's warmth
and pokey elbows
his gentle snoring
and not-so-terrible-after-all dog breath.

I pat the mattress lightly
just there
next to my leg
and hope I'll dream
he jumps up
circles
settles to sleep
beside me.

Fine, Just Fine

Next morning Sloane and I go upstairs
to the kitchen
find our parents and Mr. Bains at the table
clutching coffee cups.
They don't look at us when we come in
no *Good morning, girls*
no *How did you sleep?*
Mom finally glances up
offers a quick, tight smile.

"What's going on?" I ask.
"Is it Mike?"
Worry tangles around hope
and pulls tight
inside me.
Dad shakes his head.

It turns out
while we were sleeping in a strange bed
far from home
safe
flames leapt the asphalt line
between forest and town
and devoured

an entire neighborhood
in Pine Grove.
No one knows which neighborhood
whose houses
—the news didn't say.
But ours is on the edge of town
near the trees.

"We can only wait," Dad says,
"and hope for the best."

Mom's hands come to her face
press hard
against her cheeks
as if by pressing
she can keep hope from escaping.
She draws in a shaky breath.

"It'll be fine," she says. "We're safe
and that's all that matters."

Having our family safe
is what matters
but having a home matters too.
Having a bedroom and a kitchen
and a roof over our heads
matters.

"What about the shop?" Sloane asks.
If the mechanics' shop is lost
Dad won't have a job
to go back to

and having a job matters too.
One side of Dad's mouth quirks up
in a sad sort of smile
and he shrugs.

"And Mike?" I say
with a voice that comes out cracked
and quiet.
"What about Mike?"

Mom reaches for me
wraps me in a hug.
"I know you're worried," she says.
"I sent in the form
you filled out.
They've got Mike's description.
They've got our contact info.
Now we just have to hope
someone finds him."

Sloane turns right around
bare feet silent
on the tile floor
and strides out of the room.
Mom pushes back from the table.
"You need breakfast," she says
putting on an everything's-fine voice
that doesn't belong in this kitchen
or this moment.
She takes a cereal bowl from the counter
extends it toward me
but I don't take it.

"I want to see," I tell her.

"See?" she says.

"Pine Grove. The news."

She doesn't think that's a good idea
thinks it'll upset me
make me worry
and there's no sense worrying
about things out of our control.
That's what her words say
but her eyes scare me.
Her eyes say there's every reason
to worry
every reason
to be upset.

"You don't have to protect me," I say.

Tears spill
and she covers her mouth
with her hand.
She nods
blinks hard to stop more tears
from letting loose.

"I know," she says.
"But I still wish I could."

Imagining (again)

What if...

Mike goes to the creek
finds it dry
follows it
in search of water
runs along the creek bed
stopping to nudge a stone
with his nose
pawing at it
the way he plays with pinecones
on the path
when he runs alongside my bike...

What if...

he keeps running
keeps following the dried-up creek
like a trail
until it reaches a point
where it's not quite so dry
where it nears the river
that's bound to have water
clear and cold...

What if...

he drinks and drinks
wades right in
swims to the other side
—Mike's always loved swimming
climbs out on the far bank
safe
and lies in the shade of a birch tree
waiting for me
to catch up...

What if?

Words for Home

Jewel lies on her stomach
on the rainbow-striped quilt
chin propped on one hand
my crossword book open
in front of her.

"Five-letter word for home," Jewel says.

"House," I say automatically
without having to count
the letters.
My thoughts fly to Pine Grove.
Is my house there in the smoke
or is it gone?

"Nope," Jewel says, bringing me back
to the lime green room.
"Doesn't fit with the other letters.
Besides," she says, "*home*
doesn't have to mean a house.
I lived in a car once
and it was home."

My mouth drops open.

I snap it shut
but not quick enough
to keep Jewel from noticing.
Her freckled cheeks
blush bright pink.
She rolls over
pushes herself up to sitting
tosses the puzzle book toward me.
"Never mind," she says
looking away.

Her home
was *a car*?
It's obvious
she doesn't want to talk about it
but I need to know
—need to know it's possible
to feel at home
even if my house burns down.

"Jewel? Did you really live
in a car?"

She leans against the wall
finally looks at me.
"I know it sounds bad," she says.
"But I had my mom
and a roof over my head
—even though it was a dented
metal one."

She offers a lopsided grin.
"It worked out for a while.
And hey—I've lived in plenty of houses
since then."

"And they were home too?"

She shrugs. "The car was home
because I was with my mom.
And this place?
With the Bains?
Yeah, this is home."

"But your mom..."

"Maybe she'll be able
to take care of me again some day.
But for now, I don't have to be with her
to be home."

Maybe it's possible to be home
even without a house
but without your family?
"That doesn't make sense," I say.

"Safe is home," Jewel says. "Wanted
is home. I have that here.
And this?" She gestures
at the room. "Let's just say
it isn't a car."

She leans over
snatches the crossword book back
resumes pondering the puzzle
tapping the pencil
against her chin.

What if we live at the Bains' forever?
Or what if we live in our car
seats and floors overflowing
with the things we rescued?
And what if Mike...
what if he's not okay
if he's
gone
will I ever feel *home* again?

"Second letter is a B," Jewel says.

"What?"

"In the five-letter word
for home."

I take the book from her
stare at the squares
but no answer comes to mind.
I flip to the inside back cover
a blank space
for me to work things out.
"Words for home," I say as I write
creating the beginning
of a list.

> *HOUSE*
> *APARTMENT*
> *CAR?*

"Residence," Jewel says
so I add it to the list.
I jot down *SAFE* and *WANTED*
Jewel's words that mean home
even though they aren't actual places
to live.
I think of Heather
who lives in a condo
so I add that to the list
starting a run of words
that begin with *C*.

> *CONDO*
> *CASTLE*
> *CAVE*

Jewel laughs
at that last one.
The list grows
but nothing quite fits
the letters I need
for home.

Welcome

Last winter I did a project on pioneers
for a novel study
worked for days
on a diorama
finished the final touches
the morning it was due.
I wrapped it in a plastic garbage bag
to protect it from sleet
got it safely to class
and set it down
while I took off my coat and gloves.

Tyler Robinson sat on it.

Before I could even attempt repairs
our teacher announced a pop quiz.
Math is my best subject
but my mind
was with my flattened settlers.
We traded papers to mark them
and Heather grimaced
as she handed mine back
—my first failing mark
in Math.

Lunch was no better.
I spilled chocolate milk on my lap
snapped at Heather
when she tried to help me tidy up.
Finally the last bell rang.
I zipped my coat
shoved my math test to the bottom
of my pack
with the few salvaged bits
of my project
and reached for my gloves.
They were gone
taken by someone else
by mistake, I expect.

I trudged toward home
hands frozen despite being stuffed
into pockets
daylight already fading
stolen by dark clouds
and slushy rain.
The road seemed unusually long.

As I turned the final corner
I looked up
saw light in our kitchen window
could almost feel the warmth
and smell the cookies
I hoped Mom had baked
and my lousy day
loosed its hold on me
the tiniest bit.

A single *"woof"*
—Mike was waiting
watching.
He jumped the busted fence
when he saw me coming
rushed over
so he could greet me properly.
I dropped to one knee
soaked up Mike's welcome
and everything about my bad day
ran off me
like rainwater rushing
along the edge of the road
to the drain.

Having someone who loves you enough
to wait
in the dreary weather
someone who's happy to see you
no matter what mood
you're in...

there's nothing better
than that.

Reunion

Jewel logs onto the computer
checks the website
where she posted the picture
of Mike.
There's still nothing
—no comments
no one saying they've seen him.

"But check this out," Jewel says.
"Three chickens have been reunited
with their owner.
Chickens!" She laughs.
"Lucky the fire didn't turn them into
roasted chicken dinner."

Her joke hits
like a punch to the stomach.
"That's an awful thing to say.
The owner must've been so
worried."

Jewel's grin disappears.
"I'm sorry. I didn't mean..."

I know she didn't mean
to upset me
to put an awful thought
in my head
to make me feel worse
than ever
but that was the most
terrible
joke.

I step back from the computer
force myself to sound positive.
"Well," I say, "if chickens
can find their owners
why not dogs?"

Mrs. Bains pops into the living room
asks if we're ready to leave
for the community center.
Sloane's coming today
—not really by choice
but Mom and Dad
think she needs to do *something*
anything
besides sitting on the sofa bed
plucking the strings
of her ukulele.

When we arrive
Mrs. Bains circles the busy lot in her SUV
gives up

and parks on the street.
We cut across the dry lawn
to the main doors.
Inside, I rush to check in
with Rose Schreiber
hope trying to bubble up inside
and me forcing it down
like trying to jam a lid
on a shaken-up bottle of root beer.
When she says, "Sorry, Cara"
the hope fizzles.
Sorry, Cara means no sign of him yet
no one opened their car door
let Mike leap in
worm his way onto their lap
for the long ride to safety.
I turn away.

A woman's shriek
makes me turn back.
"Oreo! Oh, Oreo!" A tall woman emerges
from behind a row
of stacked-up small crates.
She's hugging a cat
—the black-and-white cat
who seems determined
to climb up her shirt and nestle
between her shoulder and neck.
The woman laughs and cries
and keeps on hugging.
Then Rose Schreiber points at me

and the tall woman
practically bounds across the room
with her cat
stops, breathless, in front of me.

"You rescued my Oreo?" she asks
and suddenly I'm part of the hug.
The black-and-white cat looks at me
and flicks its tail
as if to say
thanks.

The woman is happy
delighted
delirious
about having her Oreo cat back.

incredibly happy (8 letters)
E C S T A T I C

I can't stand it
for another second.

Hearts

I run from the room
leave behind the barks and meows
and happy sounds
of the Oreo reunion
and smash right into Sloane
waiting for me
in the hall.

"Watch it, Cara," she says.

Why can't she say
Hey, what's wrong?
and then I'd tell her
how much I miss Mike
how much I worry
I'll never see him again.
Instead, I push past her
find Jewel and grab her arm
stride to the large gym.
We weave between cots
to the tables at the back.

Jewel and I tear the plastic packaging
from flats of bottled water

line up the bottles
until they fill a long tabletop
so much water
a lake
standing on fold-out legs.
When we're finished
we snitch cookies from the next table
wander the room as we munch
until a familiar voice
making a not-so-familiar sound
hits my ears.

foolish or nervous laughter (6 letters)
G I G G L E

It's Sloane
standing nearby
talking to a boy.
She flips her hair
laughs again
in that very not-Sloane-ish way.
If she were a cartoon character
I swear
she'd have big red hearts
in place of eyeballs.

I elbow Jewel
jut my chin toward Sloane
and we both crack up
until I see exactly who
Sloane's acting all dopey for:

the thin man who ran out of gas
during the evacuation
with his baby girl.
Only now that I see him in good light
without smoke and ash
swirling about
I see he's awfully young
to be a dad
—probably only a few years older
than Sloane.

I quickly drum up an excuse
then barge into their conversation
ignoring the glare
I get from Sloane.

"Is your baby okay?" I ask. "The smoke
—it didn't make her sick
did it?"

"She's fine," he says
but I'm sure I see some worry
lingering
around his eyes
—or maybe
he's just real tired.
I tell him it was my dad who stopped
on the highway
and he looks at Sloane
then me
like he's figuring out a math problem.

"Sisters?" he says
then he grins. "I'm Wesley."

I'm about to ask where his baby is now
when I see Mrs. Bains coming toward us
moving in a shuffling sort of dance
side to side
holding a baby close on her chest
patting its back.
"Your Angeline sure is sweet,"
she says to Wesley. "Finally asleep too."
She squats down
beside the infant car seat
on the floor
settles Angeline without waking her
then turns to Wesley.

"Forgive me for asking," she says,
"but where's her mother?"

Wesley shrugs. "Traveling, I guess.
Or running, actually.
To be honest
I'm not sure if she's coming back."

"Who takes care of the baby
when you're at work?"

Wesley crosses his arms
leans back
on his heels.

"She's not neglected
if that's what you're thinking."

"No," says Mrs. Bains. "But I'm a mom
—I worry."
Her voice
and her expression
are gentle
and I think of what Jewel said
about being safe and wanted
and it makes complete sense
that Mrs. Bains is concerned
about Angeline.

Wesley relaxes.
"My mom takes care of her," he says.
"Or, she did
until just before the evacuation.
Her lungs are bad—got worse
with the smoke.
Now she's in hospital
here in the city
but the doctor says
she should be all right."

I figure that on top of worrying over
his mom and his baby
he's probably thinking
about the same thing
the rest of us are.

"What will you do," I ask, "if the fire...
you know...
if you lose your home?"

He says, "I try not to think about that."

There's an awkward silence
then Wesley forces a smile
crouches beside the car seat
draws a finger gently down Angeline's cheek.
Her mouth twitches
forms the tiniest smile
while she sleeps.
"But you know what?" he says softly. "This girl
has my heart.
As long as I've got her
I'm home."

That night after dinner
I open the back of my puzzle book
add to my list of words
for home:

HEART

Carry On

Rose Schreiber opens a bag of kibble
plunks it on a table
alongside a long line of bowls.
My job today
is filling the bowls
setting one in each dog's crate
while Rose stands guard
keeps the dog from coming out for a visit
latches the crate door
once I've put lunch inside.
I'm hoping for dog-walking duty
one day
or
part of me is.
The other part can hardly stand the thought
of walking a dog
who isn't Mike
not because I don't love dogs
but because I love Mike.

When I asked Rose about helping
with the animals
I thought it would be the best job ever

—miles better
than unpacking water bottles.
But it turns out
every time I walk into this
makeshift shelter
for evacuated or lost
(and found)
pets
my heart plunges to my stomach
and every time
Rose says *nothing yet*
in response to the question I ask
not with words
but with the hope that's surely written
on my face
I have to swallow my disappointment
and tend to the animals
knowing
no one's found Mike yet
knowing
he's still out there
alone.

The idea that he didn't find safety
didn't find a way out
a way to breathe...

I shove that thought away
grab another bowl
fill it with kibble
and carry on.

Fears

Whenever we have to pick teams
in gym class
I get picked last
or almost last.
It's not that I'm so terrible
at team sports
—unless it's softball
and then I really *am* so terrible.
It's just that I like the kind of sports
where nothing goes horribly wrong
if I get lost
in my daydreams—specifically
no getting bonked on the head
by a ball.

It's happened more than once
volleyball
basketball
softball.
Bonk
      bonk
            bonk.
*Soft*ball is a lie
by the way

—that one hurt way worse
than the others
so much worse
it made me afraid of playing.
So now I always duck in the back
when it's time to pick teams
glad that my size
keeps me hidden
as long as possible.

Catching a ball
isn't all it's cracked up to be
anyway.
Mike understands that
—it's why we focus on fetch
instead of catch.
After we brought him home
and he got to know me
I took him outside
with a tennis ball
tossed it to him time and time again.
Every throw
he leapt up
front legs flailing
like he was hoping to catch the ball
with his paws.
His jaw would open wide
then snap shut
closing
around nothing.

He missed that ball
every time
on account of having only one eye
to see it with
but unlike me
he was never afraid
to try.

I used to think
there were only two things
that scared Mike.
One, the yipping of coyotes
when they're too close
for comfort.
And two, the rumble of the garbage truck
which causes him to tremble
for a reason only he knows.
Both those things
make him stay close to me
—even closer
than usual.

But now I know
Mike's afraid of *three* things.

The third one is smoke.
Smoke makes him skittish
antsy to run
even if it means
          leaving my side.

Imposter

Tagging along with Jewel and Mrs. Bains
I sometimes feel like an imposter
like I'm on the wrong side
of the situation
—an evacuee
volunteering
at the evacuation center.
This afternoon Jewel and I
help sort donations of clothing
in the blue room
grouping by size
and type
jeans here
        shirts there.
Here, people who were evacuated
who have nothing
but the clothes they were wearing
and the few things
they managed to save
—here, they can shop for free
find what they need.
Even though I'm one of the people
who left almost everything
behind

I'm glad for the task
to keep my mind
off my worries.

"Can you believe
all this stuff?" Jewel says
as she empties another bag
and begins pulling random baby clothes
from the pile.

"Those should go on the table
near the door," I say.
"By the boxes of diapers."

I laugh as Jewel sticks her fingers
into the smallest pair of running shoes
I've ever seen
and makes them dance their way
into the pile.
We gather armfuls of sleepers
shirts
leggings
sized from tiny to toddler.
As we're adding them
to the stacks of kids' clothes
a cry comes from the doorway
—a woman
looking around the room
taking in all the tables piled high
with donations.

She sobs.
Another woman rushes to her side
wraps an arm around her
until the crying settles.

"Who brought all this?" the first one asks.
"Who would give all this
to strangers?"

"Everyone," the second woman says.
"Everyone did."

"I lost everything
—my house
my belongings
my clothes."
She shudders
as if one more big cry
needs to escape.
"It's all gone."

The two of them find chairs nearby
sink down side by side
then tears start
again.
"My wedding pictures
—gone.
My mother's china...
everything."

Maybe sorrow is contagious
because watching that woman's sadness
strips off my smile
my I'm-okay mask
like ripping off a bandage
leaving the wound open
for all the world
to see.

Song of Hope

In the main gymnasium
I spy Sloane
sitting on a cot
across from Wesley and Angeline
same old dopey look on her face
nodding and laughing
like Wesley's the most interesting person
in the universe.
I'm not in the mood
for laughter
or dopey sisters.

I turn around
leave the gym
and explore the hallways
of the community center.

Music
barely there
catches my attention
—a few notes
escaping from somewhere
and drifting
toward me.

I follow the sound
until I find myself
in a green room the size of my class
at school.
There's a piano against the far wall
a woman seated on the bench
her back to the room
playing
and a smattering of people
loosely gathered
listening
to the gentle melody.

I recognize the pianist
even from way over here
near the door
—Francesca Passerini
my piano teacher.
Miss Francesca lives in a house surrounded
by overgrown gardens
chock full of flowering plants
and an unusual number
of bird feeders.
Everything about her
flows
—her dark brown hair
her tunics and long skirts
the words and sentences
she speaks.
She is *legato*.

in music: smooth, flowing (6 letters)
L E G A T O

Miss Francesca eases into a new song
bright and lively
and then another
—a folk song.
There's no book open in front of her
no loose pages
lined up on the piano.
Didn't she bring her songbooks?
Doesn't she have
a just-in-case backpack
stuffed full
of sheet music?

A few people recognize
the next song.
They sing along
softly at first
eyebrows shooting up as they glance
at one another
like they'd had no intention to sing
but suddenly
the music required it.

I move closer
hovering behind others
the way I sometimes linger
on Miss Francesca's porch

after my lessons
so I can hear her play.

When she rises from the piano bench
skirt swirling
people applaud.
She graces them with a smile
which grows even brighter
when she sees me.

"Where's your music?"
I ask her.

"I suspect it's in the cabinet
beside my piano
right where I left it."

"You didn't bring it?
But what if..."

I can't say the *what if*
but she understands.

"Then I'll lose the pages," she says.
"And the piano too
I suppose. But I won't
lose the music.
It's here"
—she taps her temple
"and here"
—a tap
on her chest.

That may be true
but I can't imagine Miss Francesca
without her piano
and her pages.

"Don't look so worried," she says.
"Music
is part of me
even without instruments
and scores.
Music is where I'm most
myself.
Everyone should have that
shouldn't they?
A special place
where they can be themselves."

Two kids claim the piano bench
plunk notes randomly
and loudly.
Most of the adults wander
toward the door
contented looks on their faces
that seem at odds
with evacuations
and wildfires
and loss.

As I head back to the gym
I make a mental note
to add to the list
in my puzzle book.
I'm quite certain
music
is Miss Francesca's word
for home.

Ouch

"Cara!"

I turn when I hear my name
search the room
for the familiar face.
Heather! I hurry over to my friend
as out of place as I am
and yet both of us
belonging.
"Did you just get here?
Where were you?
Were you still in Vancouver?
I'm so glad to see you!"
She laughs as I bombard her
with words.

"We just got home
before the evacuation order
—we hadn't even finished unloading
the car.
Then my dad was helping our neighbor
with his horses
and we all went up to a ranch
that was taking in farm animals.

We stayed there
until that area was evacuated too
—and now, here we are!"

I tell her about our trip out of Pine Grove
chased by the fire
leaving Mike.
And even though I'm smack in the middle
of being happy
because I'm with Heather again
my nose prickles
eyes water.
I take a deep breath
think I'll manage not to cry
but Heather hugs me
and spills her own tears.
So much
for not crying.

I wipe my face
with the edge of my t-shirt.
"Every time I see the news
there are more fires.
I can't wait
for things to be back to normal
can't wait
for this summer
to be over."
The words won't stop.

They pour out
as if all the stress and worry
is excited to finally escape
through my mouth.
"And we'll start at McGuire Secondary!
Can you believe
we'll be in sixth grade?
Youngest at the school!"

Sixth grade used to be in Pine Grove
at the elementary school
but last year
they added on to the high school
in Braeburn
built a middle school
with a walkway that connects
right to McGuire High.
It's huge.

"Thank goodness I have you
—I can't imagine
having to walk in there
alone."

Heather's gaze drops to the gym floor.
"Actually..."

"Actually what?" I say
and even though I don't know
what she's going to say

I've got a terrible feeling
about what *actually* means.

"I don't think I'll be going,"
she says.

"But it's the only school nearby.
Unless you want to stay in Pine Grove
and redo fifth grade."
I laugh
give Heather a playful jab
with my elbow
try to make a joke
from something that feels extremely
not funny.

"I mean," she says, "I don't think I'll be going back
to Pine Grove.
My dad's talking about moving down south
to Vancouver
has been talking about it for ages
—you know.
But with the evacuation
and me changing schools
and him not knowing if he'll have a job
to go back to
he's thinking now
is the perfect time."

It's not the perfect time.
There's *no* perfect time
for leaving
your best friend.

"You can't go," I say. "What will I do
without you?"

She shrugs. "You'll have Mikaela."

Mikaela's doing French immersion.
Totally different classes.
I'll never see her.

Heather doesn't look particularly upset
about leaving me.
"My cousins are all there," she says
as if that makes it okay
to desert me.

A commotion distracts us
—her little brothers crash onto the scene
all chaos and noise and energy.
Their dad ambles along after them
says they're going to the playground
invites me
to come along.
The boys turn to me
—"Please, please, please
come with us!"
but I know they'll make us play pinch tag

which is regular tag
with pinching
instead of tagging
and they both run surprisingly fast.
It's a mean game.
We thought it was cute
when her brothers were tiny
but I guess it really wasn't.
Now, I feel like Heather's news
has already pinched me
hard enough to bruise
and once you get pinch-tagged
the only way to undo it
is to run
and pinch back.

I narrow my eyes
speak directly to Heather
say, "No thanks,"
and walk away.

Dragons

Dad perches on the arm
of an upholstered chair
while Mom and Sloane and I huddle close
on the sofa bed.
All of us focus on the TV
—the daily news update
about the fires.
An image appears onscreen
dark smoke looming
over Pine Grove.
I search for landmarks
for anything that might give a clue
about what has burned in our small town
and what is left.

The camera switches
focuses on a reporter
in front of a log building
—Pine Grove's tourist info
museum
and library
all in one.

On my eighth birthday
Sloane took Heather and me
to the park beside that building
sat on a swing
while we dashed around the wood climbing-fort
slaying dragons
with imaginary swords.
Instead of making us head home
when she got bored
Sloane became the queen
of dragon-slayers
fighting valiantly alongside her princesses
until the land was free
of fiery beasts.

Later she sat us down in the living room
painted our nails
before dinner
didn't even get mad
when I spilled her Cotton Candy pink polish
on the carpet.
Mom would've been angry about that spill
for sure
but since it was my birthday
she just frowned and cleaned it
the best she could.
Then she took a picture of us girls
Heather
          Sloane
                    me
lined up by the brick fireplace

fingers splayed in front of our grins
displaying our dragon-defeating
pink-tipped hands.

That was a long time ago
—long before evacuations
and new schools
and knots in my belly because of Mike.
How do I handle these things
without Heather
if she moves away?
How do I handle them
without Sloane
if she's no longer
on my team?

The news report carries on.
A firefighter
answers the reporter's questions
then they go to a video
of a man who refuses
to evacuate.
He's still there
armed with a garden hose
trying to save
his property.

I can't help thinking
a garden hose
isn't much of a sword.

Claddagh

Mom, Dad, Sloane, and I
drive through the city
to an outdoor market.
Both Mr. and Mrs. Bains
have to work today
and Jewel's spending the afternoon
with friends
so for the first time
since the evacuation
the four of us
are on our own.

The market is a large collection
of canopied stalls
selling baking
produce
fries, mini donuts, snow cones
and all kinds of crafts.
After agreeing to meet
in an hour
Sloane and I go one way
Mom and Dad, the other.
Sloane makes a beeline
for a stall selling handmade jewelry.

I trail behind
wait
while she browses.
I try to get interested
in the dangly earrings
which Mom would never
let me wear
but my mind keeps wandering
to Pine Grove.

"Do you think our house
is going to be okay?"

Sloane takes her time
before turning from the jewelry.
When she does
I wish I hadn't asked
the question.

"I need to *not* think about that
at least for a little while
okay?"

At the next stall
Sloane finds an infant-sized hairband
stretchy pink
with a ribbon bow.

"Angeline doesn't have much hair,"
I say.

"Doesn't matter," says Sloane
as she pays for it
and tucks it in her pocket.

"Wesley doesn't like thinking about it
either," I say. "His house, I mean.
Remember?"
Just like that
I'm back on the topic
we both hate
but can't help.
"I wonder if his house
is gone."

Sloane sighs.
"He lives in an apartment," she says.
"But I don't know. I hope not."
We step away
from the market stall.
"He'll still have Angeline
at least
and that's what counts."

I know that's what Wesley said
—that as long as he has Angeline
he's home.
Maybe there's some truth in that.
Maybe having my family
really is enough.
I think my head
almost believes it.

I just wish I knew
how to convince my heart.

We wander through the market
past tables of produce
and preserves
framed art prints
aprons with funny sayings.
Sloane pauses at another stall
selling jewelry
and a necklace catches my eye.

"This looks like Nana's ring,"
I say. "The one Mom has
on a chain."

Sloane peeks over at it
nods
and goes back to admiring
the beaded bracelets.

I finger the silver pendant
hanging from a black cord
—two hands wrap around a heart
wearing a tiny crown.
The woman behind the table
leans forward. "Ah," she says.
"That's an Irish claddagh.
It stands for love
friendship
and loyalty.

Lovely, isn't it?"

Her words stick
inside me
        love, friendship, loyalty.
They feel important
—almost urgent.
So I borrow money from Sloane
purchase the pendant
and slip it over my head.
I tuck it
beneath my shirt
and let love, friendship, loyalty
bump against my heart
the entire
rest
of the day.

Shift

Ever since smoke moved in
and draped the world
in gloomy gray
it hasn't felt like July
even though the heat
and school vacation
said it was.
But this morning the sky is
brilliant blue
and suddenly *summer*
the way it's meant to be.

I race to find Dad.
"No smoke!" I say. "Does this mean
the fires are out?"
After watching the news
again last night
I never would've guessed
the firefighters were so close
to dousing all the flames.
Now I'm ready to toss my belongings
in my pack
jump in the car

hurry home
to meet Mike.
That blue feels like hope
like maybe everything hasn't changed
maybe wildfires and smoke
and neighborhoods being devoured
didn't really happen
maybe it was all a big
horrible
nightmare.

But no.
The fires still rage.
Dad says the wind changed direction
is all
—just a shift.
But maybe now the flames will turn away
from Pine Grove.

Away from Pine Grove
means back to the forest.
Before I can stop the thought
I imagine the trees
my trees
my enormous, unending backyard
as nothing more
than a field
of ash.

I go outside
sit on the front step

fill my lungs with clean air
and force that field of ash
right out of my mind.
The wind changed
like it saw the firefighters struggling
and decided to offer them
a helping hand.
It's on our side.

The front door flies open.
Jewel grabs me
hauls on my arm
blurts out, "Come on!"

Even though I've known her
less than a week
it feels longer
like months or years were compressed
squished to fit
into five away-from-home days.
Maybe worry does that to time
or newness does
or change.
Now, she rushes me
into the living room
pushes me onto the chair
in front of the computer.
"Look."

On the screen
Mike's picture

the one we posted
and below it

a comment.

"He's been spotted!" Jewel says.

The man who commented
says he's pretty sure he saw Mike
last night
around sunset
trotting down the middle of the road
up past Rodney's Hill.

"I knew it!" I say.
"I knew he'd be okay."
Rodney's Hill isn't far
from Pine Grove.
It has to be Mike.
"Didn't I tell you he's a survivor?"

I make a million mistakes
trying to reply to the comment
too excited to type
so Jewel takes over
and we ask if he can please drive that way
again today
get Mike—Mike loves car rides.
Just please hang onto him
until I can get there
to pick him up.

Through the front window
that clear sky
catches my eye
blue and bright and hopeful.

Everything's going to be
okay.

It really is.

Wonder Woman

The community center
hosts a family fun day
for evacuated families
—burgers and ice cream
a magic show
a bouncy castle
and face painting
all happening outside
on the soccer field.
It feels like a celebration
which is strangely perfect
because even though a miserable situation
brought us here
there's so much help
so much kindness.
The volunteers look happy
about getting to know us
and I feel lighter
brighter
than I have
since we had to leave home.
Maybe this is what Mom means
whenever she tells me
to make the most

of a bad situation
—find the joy
even if it's simply the joy
of not being alone
in our troubles.

After the magic show
the four of us get ice-cream cones
and wander across the field.
I spot Heather
get the okay from Mom and Dad
to go meet her.
I don't know
what I'm going to say
but it turns out
my heart
takes control of my words.
"Are you really moving away?"

Heather nods.

"I'll miss you," I say.

"Your ice cream's dripping," she says
pointing at the cone in my hand.
Mint chocolate chip
runs over my fingers
drips on the dry ground
in little green splotches.
I lick the side of the cone
catching the worst of it

but in this heat
it's really a lost cause.
"This is disgusting," I say. "Good
but disgusting."

I toss the rest of my ice cream
in a garbage bin
and we go inside so I can wash up
in the bathroom.
On our way out
we take the back hallway
walk past a man and a woman
huddled together on a bench.
The man's bent low over his knees
head in his hands
while the woman rubs his back.
Tears
trickle down her face.

I stop.
Heather waits
pretending not to notice them.
She's always been
more polite than I
and right now I'm sure
she doesn't want to make them feel
uncomfortable.
But their sadness looks to me
like a problem that needs solving
like if all the boxes get filled in
just right

there will be an answer
and things will turn out
for the best.
"Are you okay?" I ask.
The man doesn't look up.

"We'll be fine," the woman says
which is what all adults say
when they think their problems
are too big
for kids to understand.

"Did you get evacuated?" I say.

She nods.

"Me too. And my friend."
I gesture toward Heather.
"My dog is still back there.
He got left behind."

The man shifts positions
leans against the wall
runs his hands
over his beard.

"That's awful," says the woman.

"Someone spotted him yesterday
so I'm pretty sure he's okay."
I reach for my claddagh pendant

rub it between thumb and finger.
"But I don't know
about my house."
I drop the pendant back
under my t-shirt.

"Ours..." She glances at the man
before continuing.
"Ours is gone.
It was the house my husband
grew up in
the only home
he's ever known."

The man looks at her
brow furrowed
like he's wondering why on earth
she's telling all that
to some kid
they don't even know.

"It's okay," I tell him.
"We're kind of family here.
You'll see."

The woman smiles a little.
I tell them I'm sorry
about their house
tell them there's lots of help here
tell them we'll all figure out a way
to feel at home again

eventually.
And then I stop talking
and puzzle over what I just said
because I'm not sure
it's true.
If our house is gone
I could learn to like a new place
I could get used to
a different room
a different yard
and different neighbors
but if Mike is gone
there's nowhere
that's going to feel right.

Heather and I go back outside
squint in the sunshine
wander together.
"Hey," Heather says gently
stopping me.
"I'm going to miss you
too."

We wait in line with little kids
for face-painting
get matching Wonder Woman symbols
painted on our arms.

On the outside
I'm smiling.
On the outside

I'm brave and hopeful and confident
that everything
will be okay.
But inside
—inside, I'm like the man
doubled over
on the bench.

More Imagining

What if...

Mike goes home
because even when he jumps the fence
wanders away to visit friends
I don't know about
he always comes home for dinner
every
single
day...

What if...

he waits by the door
scratches to be let in
stays
because he's patient
because he knows
I'll be there for him
as soon as I can
forces himself to wait in our yard
even though he hates the smoke
even though it hurts his eye

even though the heat
makes him feel sick
and he just
can't
breathe...

What if...

he's still there
when the flames choose our neighborhood
race from one house
to the next
climb up our walls
tear across the tinder-dry lawn—

No.

I hate this what-if story.

I shove it out of my mind
fling it far
far
away.

I will
not
think it.

Sorry

Jewel clicks over to the website
scrolls down to Mike's picture.
"Another comment!"

"Let me see."

Jewel slumps back in the chair
before I reach her side.
"Oh," she says
and I know
it's not good news.

The man went out looking
drove all over
finally saw the dog again
got that dog to hop right into his car
and took a closer look.
And he's awful sorry but
it isn't
Mike.

My hands tremble
as I type a reply:

Thanks anyway.
Hope you find the owner.

I push the chair back
stand up
walk away.
Jewel follows me
but I go into the bathroom
close the door
run water in the sink
as my hope
d
r
a
i
n
s
away.

Don't Say It

The house is sweltering.
We can't open the windows
to let in a breeze
because the smoke
is back
thick like fog
—gross
stinky
fog.
I sink into an armchair
fan myself
with my puzzle book
while Sloane lounges on the sofa
with her phone.

"Want to play cards?" I ask
wishing Jewel would hurry up
and return
from her swimming lesson.
Sloane doesn't look up
thumbs flying fast
across the screen.
"Hm?"

I guess that's a no
to cards.

Mom steps into the room
extends her cell.
"It's one of the animal shelters
returning your call."

Mom sat with me
the day I made the calls
in case they needed to speak
to a grown-up.
I called five places.
Two answered
said they didn't have him
but took the info
in case he showed up.
I left messages
with the other three
and so far
two phoned me back
no news
sorry
good luck.

Now, I reach for the phone
take the call
from the last shelter
on my list.
I listen
with fingers crossed.

No one's dropped off
a one-eyed dog.

So that's it.

No one found Mike.
No one helped him.

A weight settles over me
presses me down
tries to seep in and fill
my bones.
It takes all I've got
to reach out
and hand the phone back
to Mom.

But...

I fight back
against the heaviness
let energy rise up.

I'm not ready
will *never* be ready
to give up on Mike.

"What about other evacuation centers?"
I ask Mom. "Ones in other cities.
Ones set up
because of different wildfires."

Mike could've run a long way
before being rescued
and people wouldn't have known
he belonged here
with me.
He's probably sitting there waiting
wondering
what's taking me so long.

Mom says, "The paperwork we filled out
—it goes to all the shelters, Cara.
All the evacuation centers.
If they have him, they'll contact us."
She wraps me in a hug
says, "I'm sorry, sweetheart."

"If he's not at any of the shelters
then where is he?"

"I don't know, honey.
It's possible—"

She's going to say it's possible
Mike didn't make it out
possible
I'll never see him again
but there's no way
she's right.
I step back from Mom
interrupt
before she has a chance
to say it.

"We should be looking for him
not sitting here
doing nothing."

"You are looking
—you called the shelters
posted his picture online
you're doing everything
you can."

"*No.*" The word leaps
from my throat.
"We should be looking in Pine Grove
by the house
by the creek
by all his favorite places."

She starts reminding me
we can't go back
until the evacuation order is lifted
can't go back
even though it's our home.
I don't want to hear it.

"The stupid wildfire wrecked everything."
My voice grows louder
creeping up as if someone
has their finger on the volume switch
and won't let it off.
"Mike is who-knows-where
Heather's moving

and Sloane barely even talks to me
because she's too busy texting her
evacuation boyfriend."

Sloane throws a fierce glare at me
and I want to swallow my words
don't want her to hate me
but the words
are already out there.

Mom's eyebrows shoot up.
"Boyfriend?"

Sloane rearranges her expression
and Sweet Sloane says,
"He's not my boyfriend.
He's Wesley—with the baby girl?
Remember?"

"I should hope he's not your boyfriend,"
Mom says. "He's much too old
for you."

"He's eighteen. And he's just a friend.
I'm helping him with Angeline
—trying to be kind
to a stranger."

Oh brother.
Mom doesn't fall for it
tells Sloane in no uncertain terms

she's not to get involved
with that boy.
I almost want to tell her
that boy seems like a great guy
so in love
with his baby girl
but I'm afraid
of making things worse.

Sloane pushes past me
hisses in my ear
—"Thanks a lot."

tattletale (6 letters)
S N I T C H

Wishes

The next day
is my birthday.
It would've been nice
to wake up feeling different
feeling *eleven* or feeling *happy*
but instead I wake up
feeling crowded.
I never mind when Mike
makes himself comfortable
hops onto my bed and stretches out
taking up more than his fair share
of bed space
but I'm a little tired
of sharing with Sloane.

Mr. Bains is in the kitchen
making coffee.
He went out early
picked up cinnamon buns
for a birthday breakfast
which is a pretty nice thing to do
for a kid he hardly knows.
I maybe—*maybe*—feel a little more
birthday-ish.

Early afternoon
Mom drives Jewel and me
to the evacuation center
so we can pick up Heather
then she drops the three of us
at a movie theater.
In some ways it's better
than the sleepover I'd planned
long before I knew
we'd be evacuated
—Pine Grove doesn't even have
a theater.
But afterward
Heather doesn't want to come
to the Bains' for dinner
thinks it would be too weird
so we drop her off again
and that's it.

My birthday-ish feelings
vanish.
Instead of a sleepover
with my best friend
at my house in Pine Grove
and Mike crashing the party
stealing our popcorn
then saying he's sorry
with big slobbery dog kisses
before settling down for the night
nestled
between me and Heather...

instead of that
I'll share a sofa bed
with my sister
and Heather will spend the night
on a cot in the gym.
I don't even want to think
where Mike will sleep.

Stupid
stupid
wildfires.

After dinner
Mom and Mrs. Bains disappear
into the kitchen
come back to the dining room
with a cake
complete with eleven candles.
They set it in front of me
flames dancing.
"Make a wish," Mom says.

How am I supposed to care
about cake
candles
birthday wishes
at a time like this?

Mom prods me.
"Honey? It's your birthday
—make a wish."

"I can't," I say
and Mom's brows pull together.

Dad says, "Come on, sweetie."

But I really can't
—can't choose a wish
can't blow out the candles
can't even look
at the tiny flames
flickering on my cake.

"Just put them out," I say.

The flames dance
melt the wax
pink and purple
puddling on the icing
flames still alive
still burning
could burn the cake the house the city.
WHY
did they light them?
I push up from my chair
raise my voice.

"Put them out!"

Mom glances at Dad
and he shrugs.

Sloane leans over
blows out all eleven candles.
"Chill out, sis.
They're just candles."

It's the most she's said to me
all day.

Empty Space

"Hey," Sloane says
as I'm rummaging through my bag
at bedtime
searching
for my hairbrush
—oh where
is my hairbrush?
I turn
fumble to catch the package
she tosses at me.
"Happy birthday."

I know what it is.
She gets me the same thing
every year.

"Are you still mad at me?" I say.
"About Wesley, I mean."

She doesn't answer
just shoots me a look
that says she *most certainly is*
still mad.

"I didn't mean to tell," I say.

"Whatever.
I didn't want to date him
anyway."

I'm pretty sure
that's a lie
but I let it slide.

She grabs her bag and heads
for the bathroom
comes back in her pajamas
climbs onto the sofa bed
with her ukulele.
She strums a few chords.
"I kind of like helping
with Angeline," she says
without looking up.
"Wesley—he mostly wanted to connect
with Dad
so he could say thanks again
for stopping."

So
he didn't want to be her boyfriend
anyway.
Maybe she isn't exactly mad
after all.

Maybe she just feels bad
or awkward
about how things turned out
with Wesley.
But still
even before Wesley
she was barely speaking to me.

"Are you upset I'll be going
to your school next year?
I won't embarrass you
you know."

"You probably won't even see me," she says.
"Sixth graders and tenth graders
don't cross paths much
if ever."

"I kind of miss
how we used to be."

"Things change."

I don't want them to.
I know big sisters become teenagers
and get tired of little sisters
tagging along.
I know friends move away.
I know a small spark
can get out of control
and ruin everything.

But I wish
none of that
was true.

"I miss Mike."

Sloane laughs
startling me.
"Change the subject much?" she says.

I can't help it.
My mind
keeps going back to Mike
keeps puzzling over that empty space
in my heart.

"You going to open that?" she says.

I tear off the tissue paper
uncover
a thick paperback crossword book.
"It's perfect," I say
and she grins at me.
I push my bag out of the way
settle on the chair
and work on the kind of problems
I know
how to solve.

The Plan

Mike's been on his own
in a fire zone
for eight days.
My brain tries to get me to imagine
what I'll do
if I get bad news
how I'll feel
if I never see him again
but my heart shoots messages right back
whispering
don't give up
don't give up
don't give up.
I'm not sure whether those messages
are for me
or for Mike.

I need to know if he's alive.
Even if someone finds him
takes him in
and then won't give him back
that would almost be okay
as long as I know
he's safe.

The not-knowing
feels like being locked away
in a room with no windows.
Fire or no fire
I need to get out
need to see for myself
go to Pine Grove
search for Mike
in the places I know
better than anyone.

"Do you think there's a bus?" I ask Jewel.
She's lived here two years
so she must know.
She types something into the computer
searches
while I wait
and hope.

"It's only twice a week," she says.
"But even those are canceled
until the evacuation order
is lifted."

"There must be a way."

"Welll..." Jewel draws out the word
stretching it until it sounds
like possibility.
She waggles her eyebrows
hinting at something big.

"What? Tell me!"

"I know someone
with a driver's license," she says.

I'm still missing a piece of this puzzle
need another clue
an extra letter.

"She also has a car."

Bingo.

Turns out Jewel had a foster sister
at the place she used to live.
"I was always in trouble
with the parents," she says,
"but Nat and I
—we got along great."

Could this really work?
"Find out
if she'll take me."

"Take us, you mean," Jewel says
and it feels good
to have a teammate
someone who understands
this must be done.

A Change of Plans

Today is Natalie's day off
from her job at the Dairy Queen
and so it's also
finally
the day I'm going to find
Mike.

Dad and Mr. Bains are in the boys' room
tapping tiny nails
into new baseboards.
I hover in the doorway
half in
half out
tell Dad we're off to visit Jewel's
sort-of sister.
It's a sort-of truth
a part of the truth.
My stomach thinks *part of the truth*
isn't truth at all
and our plan tangles
inside me.
My lips pinch closed
to keep the whole story

from wandering out and ruining
everything.

Mr. Bains glances at the time.
"Home for dinner?" he says.

"We'll probably eat with Nat,"
says Jewel
not sounding at all
like stories and half-truths
are trying to tumble out.

Dad's brows pull down
in a way that suggests
he's not especially keen
on this idea.
"Please, Dad?" I say. "We'll be home
before dark."
Can we get to Pine Grove
find Mike
return to the city
before dark?
The days are summertime long
but even summertime days
come to an end.
After a quick look at Mr. Bains
a silent exchange
Dad says okay.

"See you later!" Jewel says
ushering me away from the door frame

down the hall
out the front door
before I can blurt out anything
that will wreck our plan.
We've barely made it to the sidewalk
when a door bangs
behind us.
A few seconds later
Sloane grabs my arm
stops me
in my tracks.

"Where are you really going?"
she says.

"To see Natalie," I say
my voice catching
in my scratchy throat.
I wave a hand in front of my face
as if it'll help clear
the smoky air
or obscure
the truth
but of course
it does neither.

"Yeah, right," Sloane says.
"I saw the looks you and Jewel
have been giving each other.
You're up to something."

I yank my arm free
stare at the crack
in the sidewalk
while I figure out
what to say next.

I risk the truth.

"We're going to Pine Grove
to find Mike."

"And how do you expect
to get there?" she says.

As if in answer
a beat-up blue car
pulls to the curb and stops
just ahead of us.

"There's Natalie," says Jewel.
"Let's go."

I look from Jewel
back to Sloane.
"Don't tell Mom and Dad.
Please.
I have to do this."

"You blabbed to Mom
about Wesley."

Would she really tell
just to get back at me?

"Give me one good reason
I shouldn't tell," she says.

Tears prick at my eyes.
I look at Sloane straight-on
willing her
to understand.
"Mike," I say.
"Mike is a very
good
reason."

Her expression changes.
Maybe I've convinced her.
Maybe our plan
isn't ruined.

"I'm going with you,"
she says
and I open my mouth
to protest.
"I'm going with you
or I'm telling."

The Fire Zone, part 1

Sloane strides to the house
opens the door
hollers to let Dad know
the change of plans.
When she returns, I ask
what she said to him.
"Relax," she says.
"I just told him I was bored
so I was going with you.
He doesn't know."

We climb into Nat's car
Jewel up front
Sloane and me in back.
Jewel introduces us
then Natalie grins at her.
"So," Nat says, "tell me.
What's the secret mission?"

"We need to rescue a dog,"
says Jewel. "Her dog."
She jabs a thumb
in my direction.

"A most noble mission,"
Nat says. "And I take it
that dog
is in Pine Grove?"
She looks at me
in the rearview mirror
sees me nod.
Then she pulls away from the curb
drives down the road
and heads out of the city.

Last time I was on this highway
it was packed with traffic
everybody leaving
running
for their lives.
Today, it's empty.
We've been on the road now
less than an hour
but it feels as though we're a thousand miles
from anywhere.
Sloane stares out the side window.
Is her stomach as jumpy
as mine?
Jewel and Nat chatter away
catching up with each other's lives.
When the road veers left
and the view changes
they get quiet.
Ahead, black and gray remnants of forest
mar the hills.

This does not look
like the way home.

feeling of foreboding (5 letters)
D R E A D

A little farther on
a cluster of pine trees
stands untouched
but in the distance
flames
where a section of forest
still burns.
My mouth goes dry
pulse races.
Natalie glances at Jewel
grips the steering wheel tight.
"You sure about this?" she asks
tossing the words over her shoulder
to me.
No, I'm not sure
not the least bit.
What if it gets worse
up ahead?
What if sparks are still flying
debris still falling
on the road?

I can't let fear
get the best of me now.

"It'll be fine," I say.
"I saw on the news
the firefighters
have it mostly under control."
I saw nothing
of the sort
but it possibly could be
true.

We drive in silence
finally pass a mileage sign
—not too much farther
to Pine Grove.
Here, the trees are still standing
still green
underbrush hugging the edge
of the highway.
"See?" I say.
"It's not as bad here."
I mean the words
to sound strong
certain
but my voice
is barely more than a squeak.

From my spot behind Jewel
I lean forward to peer
through the windshield
scan the bush, the shoulders, the road
        from one side

to the other
       and back
trying to make Mike appear
by watching
and hoping.

We must be nearly there.
We round a curve
and Natalie slows the car.

"Uh-oh," she says.

Still Imagining

What if...

Mike runs
because he's scared
or because he knows
how dangerous it is
to stay at home
so he runs
through the forest
dodging sparks and debris
flung by the fire
runs and runs and runs
until he's deep in the woods
so deep
he can't find his way out
again...

What if...

he crosses paths
with coyotes
the same pack who attacked before
and maybe the flames change things
create a truce

among the animals fleeing
and Mike joins the pack
and keeps on running
or maybe
the flames change nothing
and the coyotes attack
again...

What if...

I never
see him
again?

The Fire Zone, part 2

To our left
the forest is gone
charred trunks smoldering
in a wasteland.
Ahead of us
an orange and black barrier
blocks the road.
A police car is parked facing us.
The door opens
and an officer steps out
wearing reflective gear
and fastening a special mask
over her nose and mouth.

"Is there another way to your town?"
Natalie asks
as the police officer takes a few steps
toward us.
Sloane speaks up
surprising me.
"Hector Road," she says.

Of course! The dirt road
I bike on.

It goes up to the viewpoint
but it also winds around back
behind the town
wanders past rural properties
crosses the creek
on a narrow bridge.
I never bike beyond the creek
but I'm pretty sure that old road
is the one that meets up
with the highway
west of Pine Grove
pretty sure Dad's taken that route
and pretty sure
we can find it.

"We must've passed it already,"
I say.

Natalie makes a U-turn
waves to the officer
zooms back
the way we came.

We almost miss it.
"There!" Sloane calls out
and Nat hits the brakes.
The road is nothing more
than two dirt tracks
separated by yellow tufts
of grass.

Overgrown brush makes it barely visible
from the highway
and no sign
marks its existence.

I lower my window.
Smoke hangs in the air
winds among the trees
sneaks into the car
as we crawl along
bumping through potholes.
Except for the engine noise
of Natalie's car
it's awfully quiet
not even a crow complaining
about our presence.
I scan the trees
watch for movement
search for a hint
of rust-colored fur.

Another barricade greets us.

"Oh no," I say.

"Got a Plan C?" Nat asks.

Jewel twists around in her seat
raises her eyebrows
asking me
what we should do.

No one's in sight
no police car
no officer to send us away.

"I got this," Sloane says
before I can answer.
She hops out of the car
drags the barrier to one side
so we can pass.
She coughs
pulls the neckline of her shirt
over her nose
and runs back to the car.

The road climbs to a ridge
curves back on itself
and the view opens up
—more flames
far in the distance
swallowing the forest.
My heart pounds
chest squeezes with the memory
of leaving
of heat and smoke and fire
driving us out
but I can't run
—not this time.
I can't desert Mike
again.

A break in the trees below
—is that the bridge?
"Stop!" I say.
I'll search on foot
call out for him
he'll hear my voice
he'll come out
from wherever he's holed up
waiting.

The smoke claws its way into my lungs
and it takes all I've got
to yell for Mike
to run along one of the dirt tracks
calling
        calling
                calling.

"Mike!
Mike Wazowski!
Mike!"

I hear Jewel and Nat
and Sloane
calling behind me
helping me search.

I need to get to the creek
to our neighborhood
to my yard.

A pickup truck rumbles into view
coming toward me.
It stops
and for a moment
I freeze.
A man in the driver's seat
lifts a phone to his ear.
He talks a little
then tosses the phone aside
hops out of the truck
and starts in my direction.

The Fire Zone, part 3

I zip off the road
into the underbrush
aiming to get past him
without having to answer any questions
but he's fast
for an old guy
is in front of me before I know it
grabs my arm.

I'm caught.

"Keep going," I yell back to the others
but they stumble to a standstill
behind me.
The man loosens his grip
lets me go.

"You girls can't be here,"
he says.

"*You're* here," Sloane says
a twig snapping underfoot
as she moves closer
—so close her arm brushes mine.

The man's gaze jumps to her
then takes in the four of us
standing there with hands or shirts over our mouths
trying to keep out the worst
of the smoke.

"I'm on my way out," he says finally,
"and you should be too."

My fingers go to the black cord
around my neck
the pendant warm
against my skin
and I explain about Mike
how I never should've left him
how we all had to leave
in a hurry.
But...

"Why didn't you leave?" I say
as my hand drops
to my side.
"When the order came
we only had ten minutes."

"I had horses to move out,"
he says.
"A barn to save
or try to
at any rate."

He doesn't look like the man
on the news
the one with the garden hose.
How many people
stayed behind?
Could *we* have stayed?
Could we have waited
for Mike?

"The police let you stay?" I ask.

He grunts
then jerks his head
in the direction of the road.

"Certainly not gonna let *you* stay."

A police officer steps off the dirt road
pushes through the underbrush
toward us.

"That was quick," the man says.

"I was in the neighborhood,"
says the officer
with a trace of a smile.
She's not wearing the mask now
but I'm pretty sure
she's the one we ran into
on the main road.
She followed us?

"Why are you still here, Jake?"

"Just as well I was," he says,
"or you'd be traipsing through the bush
tracking down these young ladies yerself."

The officer signals us
to get going
back toward Nat's car.
She pauses
side-eyes Jake
says, "No barn's worth losing your life for."

"My dad built that barn," Jake says.

"Jake—"

He holds up his hands
like he's trying to stop
whatever words she's about to say.
"I'm leaving," he says.
"Don't you worry.
Lightning started three new fires
last night
—one of 'em too darn close
for my liking.
I know when it's time to fight
and when it's time
to throw in the towel."

"All right," the officer says.
"Thanks for the call.
You keep safe now."

She marches the four of us girls
back to Natalie's car.
The squad car is parked behind it.
The officer takes our names
examines Nat's ID
says she'll be calling our parents
and we'd better not take any more detours
on our way
back to the city.

"My sister's dog," Sloane says.
"He might be out here.
Just give us a few minutes."

The officer shakes her head
points to Nat's car.
"Go," she says.

"But her dog—"

The officer's expression softens.
"I'll keep an eye out.
But you girls
—go."

As Natalie maneuvers the car
getting turned around
on the narrow road
I sag against the back seat.
Sloane pulls me toward her.
I slump over
head on her lap
helpless
and hopeless
as I abandon Mike
all over again.

Gone

Mom scolds
lectures
cries.
Dad tries to smooth things over.
Jewel is banished to her room
for the rest of the evening.

When the dust settles
I retreat to the family room
find my crossword puzzle book
focus on filling in boxes.
But my mind
keeps going back
to driving away
leaving again
failing.

My misery and my quiet space
are invaded
when Mom and Dad come in
armed with fake cheerfulness
and Sloane
wanders in after them
not faking anything.

Dad borrowed a Monopoly game
from the Bains
insists it's just what we need.

"Put down the puzzle book, Cara.
Phone away, Sloane.
Family time!"

Sloane and I both know
there's no point in fighting
family time.
The four of us cram onto the pullout bed
set up the board
and pretend
to relax.
To be honest
I'm glad to have something
to distract me
because the puzzles
weren't working.
The longer our Monopoly game goes on
the better.

We've been playing
at least an hour
when Dad's cell rings on the end table.
He leans over
looks at the screen
face changes
and he fumbles to answer.
Dad's jaw tightens
as he listens.

He nods
as if whoever's on the phone
can see him
then his voice
strangled-sounding
like the words would rather not be said
at all.

"I understand...
No...
Yes...
Thank you for letting me know."

He gets up and walks out of the room
without a word.
Mom stands
doesn't look at us
says, "Stay here"
and follows Dad.

Sloane gathers the houses
and hotels
from the board.
"I want to keep playing," I say
but Sloane gives a curt shake of her head
glances at the doorway.
"We're done," she says
and I get the feeling she knows something
I don't.

"What's going on?" I say.

She doesn't answer
sorts colorful paper money
into the proper slots
slides the lid into place
just as Mom and Dad step into the room
serious looking
and quiet.
Mom's nose is red
like she's been crying
or is about to.
She holds out her hands
telling us to come close
and the four of us
cluster together
in the Bains' family room.

Dad draws in a deep breath.
"That phone call," he says
then he hesitates.
"I'm sorry, girls.
The fire
—our house
is gone.
Probably nothing left
but it'll be at least a week
before we can go see
for ourselves."

Smoke and Water

That night I dream
we're living in our car.
I'm sleeping
on the floor
Nana's rescued quilt
tucked around me
five or six or seven
black-and-white cats
crowding in
vying for a corner of quilt
and the smoke
—the smoke seeps
through cracks in the floor
creeps in the edges of the windows
stings my eyes
and water
—water comes
to wash away the smoke
pours in
until I wake up in the dark
sunshine happy-face night-light
glowing
and tears streaming
onto my pillow.

I hate bad dreams

and I really need to know
I don't have to live
in the car.

The River

We must've used up all our tears
last night
because today
all of us have dry eyes.
We move like there's no strength
in our bones
barely speak
as if the smoky air
finally stole our voices.
The Bains say how sorry they are
about our house
and then they don't say much else
at all.
Are they wondering if perhaps we'll stay
forever?

The wind has shifted again
leaving the day bright
and cheerful
which is the exact opposite
of how it should look.
Mom decides we need to go out
get some fresh air

take advantage
of the smoke-free sky
while we have it.
Mrs. Bains tells us about a park
by the river
—picnic area
walking trails
and if we're lucky
a mobile pie shop
where we can buy dessert
after our lunch.
I can't see how a picnic
and pie
will make me feel any better
about having no home.

"It'll be fun," Mom says
looking like someone cut a big paper smile
from a glossy magazine
pasted it
onto her face.
I don't remember the last time
we picnicked back home
not sure we ever did
but Mom says, "Of course we did!
And besides, you're never too old
for a family picnic."

Sloane looks like she disagrees
but doesn't say so
actually helps Mom pack the lunch

and the four of us get in the car
that I hope is not our home
and we zip across town
Mom driving
Dad with the map open on his phone
directing.

The parking lot's busy
and sure enough
a food truck is set up
serving window open
and a swarm of people
buzzing around it.
We skirt the crowd
with our container of sandwiches
and bottles of iced tea
climb a small hill
come upon a garden of flowering shrubs
and the beginning
of a bark-mulch trail.
The trail leads us to a cluster
of picnic tables
alongside a river
sunlight dancing on its surface
like fireflies
flitting about at night.

It feels magical
for about two seconds
until I stumble on a root
land on my knees
in the bark.

Stupid trail.
I'd rather have my dirt road
my bike
my dried-up creek
—but why, oh why
doesn't that dumb old creek
have at least a trickle
of cool water
for Mike?
How is he supposed to know
to follow it
and keep following until dust
meets dampness
and he finally finds
a drink?
I haul myself up
brush off hands and knees
then aim a ferocious kick
at the trail
sending bits of bark
flying.
Mom tells me to relax
and enjoy the day.

How can I
when our home is gone?
When Mike
is still out there somewhere
alone?

A question drifts into my thoughts.

I don't want to know the answer
but I ask anyway.
"How many days
can a dog go without water?"

Before anyone can respond
I take it back.
"Never mind.
I'm sure he found water.
He's a very smart dog.
He's a survivor."

I have to get back there
and try again.
I know the house is gone
everything's gone
the fire
is still too close
but Mike
—he might still be out there
waiting.

Dad should phone that guy back
tell him we can't wait a week
tell him we're going now
packing up our picnic
and high-tailing it
to Pine Grove.
I bet if Mom and Dad went with me
that police officer
would let us through.

"Please
please
let's go back
let me look
again."

Mom pulls me down beside her
on a picnic bench
keeps holding my hands
like she's afraid I'll fly away.
"It's been almost two weeks, Cara.
I think you need to understand
there's a good chance
we won't find him.
The odds of him surviving..."

Her eyes say Mike's gone
give up
there's just no way.

My words try to choke me
but I force them out.
"I *will* find him," I say.
"I have to.
He's Mike Wazowski.
Mike Wazowski
doesn't die."

More tears
—how are there any left
inside me?

But there are more
so many more
and I hate that I can't stop them.
They run right off my face
run like the river
gurgling beside us
a soggy
     snotty
          just-won't-stop
river.
Mom tries to pull me in
but I twist away.

"Let her have hope,"
Dad says to Mom.
"What else
have we got left?"

His voice
is an empty room.
Instead of making me feel better
it hollows me out
until every last bit of hope
drifts away
with the current.

          absence of hope (7 letters)
             D E S P A I R

Huckleberry Pie

We make our way back
to the parking lot
queue up
at the pie truck.
When it's our turn
Mom buys two whole pies
to give to the Bains
and four slices of huckleberry
for right now.

We sit on the prickly grass
away from the crowd
and eat together.
Even though Mike is gone
our house is gone
everything
is gone
and even though
I'm completely miserable
still, something about this moment
feels right
and familiar.
Not that we've ever before sat on dried-up lawn
behind a food truck

devouring pie with plastic forks
after our lives fell apart
but the eating together
the not really saying much
but meaning a lot
together
—that almost feels
like home.

Almost.

I scrape up the last bit
of the sweet, purple filling
and lick off my fork.
When I look up
Dad's got his empty plate balanced
on his head
and his fork sandwiched
between his nose
and his bunched-up top lip
—a hat
and a white plastic mustache.
It's not funny
and yet
it is.

"Very attractive, Dad,"
says Sloane
with a straight face
and then

at exactly the same time
laughter bursts from the two of us
so much laughter
I can't stop
and my stomach hurts
and my eyes leak
and, oh my goodness
I almost feel bad
about being happy for a minute
but it feels so good
to let some of that stress and tension
escape.

Pinpricks

I keep thinking of things
I've lost
and each new remembrance
hurts
one pinprick after another.
How many holes
until my heart leaks out?
How many holes
until I fall apart?

The framed picture of me and Heather
after our school play last year
—Heather cross-eyed
and me giving her bunny ears
both of us hyper and exhausted
at the same time.
If I'd known that would turn out to be
the last school play we'd do together
I'd have put that photo
in my just-in-case backpack.

The kaleidoscope
Sloane brought back for me

from her class trip
to Science World
two years ago.

My books
all my books.
Will I get in trouble
for letting my library books
burn up?
I wasn't even finished reading them.

Poke
        poke
                poke

ouch
        ouch
                ouch.

"What are you most sad about losing?"
I ask Sloane.

"That's a weird question."

"It's just...I can't stop thinking
about what's gone.
Besides the house, I mean."

Besides
Mike.

A panicky ball of emotion
balloons inside me.
I swallow hard
force it down.

Sloane shrugs
looks at the ground.
"It's stupid," she says.

"What? Come on. Tell me."

She hesitates.
"Remember that old stuffie
I've had since forever?"

"You mean Patches?
You still have him?"

Her expression twists.
"Not anymore."

Farewell

The next days are a strange mix
of knots in my belly
and belly laughter
worrying, waiting, wondering
bad Dad-jokes
and goofing around with Jewel
minutes taking forever
and whole afternoons passing suddenly
so that almost without warning
we're packing
to go home.

"Where will you live?" Jewel asks.

"There's a hotel," I say.
"We'll stay there for a while
then maybe we'll find
an apartment."

Should I add *hotel*
to my list of words for home?
The news said it could be a year
or more

before life is back to normal
in Pine Grove
before houses are rebuilt
new routines
are found.
I'm not sure we'll last a year
to be honest.
So much is up in the air
a mystery.
Maybe it'll work out
but maybe
it won't.

"Who knows," I say. "Maybe we'll move
to the city. Then I can see you
again."

"That'd be good," she says.
"But Natalie and I do know the way
to Pine Grove."

I want to thank her for that day
for helping me search
for caring
about Mike
but the words jam up inside me.

"The website," I say instead.
"I haven't...
I should look once more
before we leave."

"I checked," Jewel says.
"Last night.
This morning."
She shakes her head.
"Sorry."

"Okay. Well..."
Don't cry don't cry don't cry.
"Thanks."

I collect my backpack
and the bag of things I've acquired
since we were evacuated
—extra clothes
Mom bought me
my new toothbrush
birthday presents
and the happy-face night-light Mrs. Bains insisted
I take
because she bought it especially
for our visit.

It's strangely difficult
saying goodbye
to this family we've known
only two and a half weeks.
Mrs. Bains hugs each of us
and Mr. Bains reminds us
twice
that if we ever need a place to stay
we are welcome
in their home.

Another World

It seems to take forever
and no time at all
to reach the turnoff for Pine Grove.
I've wanted so badly
to be here again
to know
to see for myself
the truth of all that happened
but now that we're close
I wish time would
stop.

Just as I feared
the forested hills
where I used to ride my bike
are now fields of ash
shot through with black spikes
that once were evergreens.
This isn't my world
not the place I grew up
—it can't be.
Another world
another time

maybe another planet
all black and gray and silent.
Will plants grow again?
Will trees?
Where are the deer and the ravens?
When will I hear coyotes barking again?
How will the air
get back to being clear
and clean
and sweet?

The Welcome to Pine Grove sign signals us
says this really is the place.
The ash covering the top of the sign
looks like a thick coat of
dirty white paint.
Sloane pulls out her earbuds
sets her phone on the seat.
Dad takes a hand off the steering wheel
reaches for Mom.
They share a quick glance
then Dad focuses on driving again.
We slow down as we make our way
through town
barely moving at all
as we near our neighborhood.

"Let's walk from here," Mom says
so Dad parks the car
and the four of us get out.

A heavy haze still blankets the area
the air still scratches
on its way into my lungs.
The burned-out skeleton of a school bus
lies just ahead on the road
no tires
no seats, as far as I can tell.
Just a shell.
"How am I going to get to school?" I say.
Sloane shoots me a look
that says it's a stupid question
but she says nothing.

We turn a corner
and freeze.
Ahead of us
temporary fencing stands on metal feet
planted
on the sidewalks
running along both sides of the road.
Beyond it
nothing but wreckage
rubble.
This couldn't possibly have been
a neighborhood.

Shirts pulled up to cover our noses
we walk silently along the remains of the street
shuffling through ash
and bits of debris.

We turn right
on what I *think* is our road.
How can I not be sure?
I've lived here my whole life.
"Is this—" I start to ask
and Mom nods.
The lopsided fencing blocks access
to the piles of rubble
that once
were houses.
Three down on the left
we come to a standstill
and stare.

There's nothing.

Nothing that resembles a home
a house
a roof over our heads.

Ashes

A tower of bricks
rises
from a sea of rubble
—the chimney.
Dad's pickup
gray and hollow like the bus
sits on its axels
in our driveway.
A large scorched box
catches my eye
—the dryer, Dad tells me
and I imagine the laundry room
shiny white washer and dryer
and two blue emergency bins
stacked in the corner.
The bins still sit in the trunk
of Mom's car
beside the laundry basket half full
of canned food.

Is this real?
And the day we got the order
to evacuate
—was *it* real?

Loading those bins
my just-in-case backpack
brushing Mike in the backyard
riding my bike
on the trails...

I scan the wreckage.

There
—there, where our busted-up fence
used to be
there, half-buried in debris
almost right where I'd left it
the day of the evacuation order
—I see it
red paint cooked right off
wheels ravaged
handlebars barely recognizable.
My bike.
My got-it-early-to-enjoy-during-summer-vacation
birthday present.

Sloane's hand bumps mine
takes hold.
I look at her
follow her gaze
know that *she* knows
what I'm looking at.
She squeezes my hand
before letting go.

My eyes sting.
Whether from the air
or the bike
or the weight of everything
I don't know.

"We'll be okay," Dad says
without taking his eyes off our
used-to-be house.
He has an arm around Mom's waist.
His other hand comes up and settles
on Sloane's shoulder
and in turn
Sloane pulls me close.
Dad says, "I know this is..."

He hesitates
and Mom finishes his sentence.
"Heartbreaking," she says.
"It's heartbreaking."
Silent tears stream
from her eyes.

Dad nods. "But we're safe,"
he says. "And we'll be okay."

Is he trying to convince us
or himself?
For a moment I'm back
in the Bains' family room

Monopoly game abandoned
the four of us standing together
in the wake
of awful news.
It was terrible
and this is worse
—miles worse.
But we're standing
together.

"I can't believe it's all gone,"
Mom says.
"Everything we worked for."

It still feels like another world to me
a scene
from a movie.
Looking around, I know
Mom was right
my worries were right:

there are no dogs
in a place
like this.

A hot breeze blows my hair into my eyes
forces filthy air into my lungs.
I cough
then pull up the neck of my t-shirt again
and turn my back
on the ugly truth.

I need to think of other things
—*any* other things.
Before me
the whole fence-lined block
is in ruins.
What about Heather's condo
a block over?
Is it okay?
And Mikaela's house? And the shop
where Dad works?
How is life ever
going to be normal again?

We walk slowly back to our car.
They said it would be weeks yet
before it's safe
to get a closer look at our property
weeks before we can look through the rubble
for anything
that might be saved.

I can't imagine
there's anything worth saving
at all.

What Remains

Where do we go
if we have no home?

Where do we belong
if there's no place
that's ours?

A room in a hotel
or an apartment
strange and bare
can never take the place
of the house
we've lived in
forever.

I'm like a balloon
cut loose
drifting
and lost.

We walk past another fenced-off spot
where nothing but a brick chimney
remains.

How strange
that the rooms where a family lived
shared celebrations
and sadnesses
big moments
and boring days
how strange
that those walls are gone
and the only thing left
to bear witness
to the lives lived there
is a towering
stack
of bricks.

But maybe
home is like that
—our house is gone
and my sweet Mike
is gone
but maybe there's something that remains
through it all
like if Wesley has Angeline
Miss Francesca still hears music
in her heart
Heather is with her relatives
and Jewel is safe
and wanted.
But what is it
for me?

There are so many words
on the list
inside the back cover of
my crossword book
heart
music
family
safety
and even that five-letter word
Jewel had to cheat
and look at the answers in back
to figure out
abode.
What kind of word for home
is that?
But if *car* belongs on the list
well...I guess *abode* works too.

I bet if you asked one hundred people
you'd probably find
there are one hundred words
for home.
Turns out
home isn't always with family
but often it is.
It isn't always a place
but sometimes it is.
It isn't always within your grasp
but when you find it
you know to
hold on.

Color

When we pass the school bus again
Sloane nudges me
and finally responds
to my question:
"I don't know how we'll get there," she says.
"But we'll go together
okay?"

Everyone else gets in the car
but I hesitate
door open.
I need one more look
one more moment
to take in the rubble and destruction.
I scan the mess.
Everything
wears such a thick coat of ash
it's as if all color was erased
from the neighborhood.

All color except...

I squint
focus on a flash of movement

a glimpse of orangey-brown.
My heart picks up its pace
thuds in my chest
but why?
What am I seeing?
Something expands within me
fills me up
propels me away from the car
toward the movement
the color.
It can't be
but oh! it must be.
Please, oh please
let it be.
My legs stretch out
running now
feet pounding ash-white pavement
and I know
—I *know*

it's Mike.

Rusty fur
tongue lolling
racing straight for me.
I drop to my knees
bare skin rough asphalt
arms wrap
around his neck.
His tail waves wildly
whole back-end dances

raising dusty clouds around us
so I'm coughing
and laughing
and crying
and Mike is here
and it's all leaps
and licks
and so
much
love.

Help and Hope

The vet wants to keep Mike
overnight
give him IV fluids.

After the wagging and wiggling
settled
it was clear
Mike needed help.
He was tired and weak
not his usual self
at all.
I could feel his ribs
when I hugged him.
The vet said it was clear
he'd found a water source
but he was still dehydrated.
"Some IV fluids
and a few good meals,"
she said, "and he should be fine."

Now, the vet and my Dad wait
for me to let go
of Mike's leash

so the vet can get started
with the IV.
"I'm not leaving," I say.

"It's just one night," the vet says.
"I know you've missed him
but it's only one more night."

One more night
is not okay.
Leaving him again
is not okay.
My fingers tighten around the leash.
"I said, I'm not leaving."

Dad steps close
puts his hand on my shoulder
and doesn't say a word.
Together
he and I outwait the vet
until finally she steps from the room
to call the tech
who'll be working overnight.
The tech agrees
to let me and Dad stay.
Mom brings us dinner
nabs pillows and a blanket
from the hotel room
and that night
Dad sleeps in a chair
dragged in from the waiting room

and I make a bed on the tile floor
as close to Mike's kennel
as the tech allows.
When she's not looking
I move it a smidge closer.

In the morning
Mike looks better
but Dad
looks a wreck.
We go to the hotel
where Sloane and Mom spent the night.
Dad takes one bed
I take the other
and even though
Mike's probably not supposed to
he climbs right up beside me
reminding me
he's always thought of himself
as a lap dog.
He makes himself comfortable
and I drift off to sleep
nose to nose
with Mike.

I wake later to snuffling sounds
discover Mike snooping
in my backpack.
He pulls out Flopsy
but knows
not to dare chew on her

just drops her on the carpet
and sticks his head
back into my bag.
"What are you after?" I say.
A moment later
he comes up
with his favorite toy.
It seems like forever ago
I packed it for him
just
in
case.

After we've all eaten lunch
—peanut butter and banana sandwiches
made on the tiny
hotel-room table
I fasten Mike's leash
and we all head out
for a walk.

We walk past the mechanic shop
which is still standing
—the fires didn't touch anything
along that whole block.
The library-museum-information center
didn't burn down either
and it seems that now
more than ever
it's the hub of Pine Grove.

People wander in
stop to talk
ask how their neighbors
are faring.
Mike greets each one of them
with an enthusiastic
tail wag.
The guy working there today
doesn't mind Mike
being inside
but who would mind
a sweet-natured
one-eyed dog
doing his very best
to make everyone feel welcome?

A bulletin board holds offers
of places to stay
families who didn't lose their houses
in the fire
sharing with those of us
who did
—a basement suite
a spare bedroom
a travel trailer in the backyard.
Dad snaps photos
of several offers
storing the info
so he can call later.

Donations of food and clothing
and pretty much everything else
I can think of
fill the hallways
free for the taking
for anyone in need.
Here, like at the evacuation center
there's so much kindness.
It doesn't bring back our house
but it does bring help
and hope
and a belief
that we really will be
okay.

comfort during hard times (6 letters)
S O L A C E

Home

Sloane and I take Mike to the park
beside the info center.
The wood climbing-fort
is a bit rundown these days
but it's still a fine place
to fight dragons.
I let Mike off leash
to explore.
"You stay close," I tell him
but I don't need to say it.
It's clear
Mike has no intention
of letting me out of his sight
anytime soon.
He lies down nearby
and watches me.
I sit on a swing
next to Sloane
push with my toes
swing just high enough
to create a breeze
and slice through
the summer heat.

"Do you think we'll stay
in Pine Grove?" I ask.

"I don't know," says Sloane.
"Dad still has a job, at least."

The haze
hanging over the town
is thinner
less choking
than when we left
but it stinks of burnt trees
burnt houses
burnt cars.
One hundred and forty buildings
were lost to the fire
including our house
and all our neighbors'
Heather's condo
and the corner store
at the end of our road.
The news said
if it wasn't for the hard work
of the firefighters
all of Pine Grove
would've been gone.

I push harder
lean back
pump my legs.

I swing higher
and higher
until I feel the lift
in my belly
then the

  drop

as I whoosh
through the air.
My claddagh pendant thumps lightly
against my chest.

Love (thump).

  Friendship (thump).

    Loyalty (thump).

My family
arms around each other
staring at the ashes of our house
together.

  Sloane
  on my team again
  —or maybe
  she always was
  and just didn't know how
  to show it.

And Mike
who waited
and watched
because he knew
I would come.

The pieces fall in place
like one letter
after another
filling in the boxes
and fitting
just right.
Love
friendship
loyalty.

All my mixed-up feelings
rush together inside me
whoosh
right along with the swing.
I let go

    l e a p

       s o a r

land
on the patchy grass.

Maybe there's a word
for this claddagh feeling
of love and friendship and loyalty

of knowing I'm not alone
knowing someone's got my back
when I need it
knowing someone
(or some dog)
won't give up on me
just like I won't give up
on him.
Maybe there's one word
I can add to the top
of my list
one word that wraps it all up
so I can tuck it away
in my heart
and find it there
whenever I'm feeling alone
or adrift.

I could call it "claddagh"
but maybe
I don't need a new word
for what home is
for me.
Maybe I don't even need
my list
because it turns out
I haven't lost home at all
—I'm just finally figuring out
what it is.

Mike stands up
bounds over

as I brush dirt from my hands.
Sloane ruffles his fur
then dashes to the fort
slaps her thigh
so Mike will follow her up the ramp
over the clatter bridge
to the platform
—I'm positive she loves him
more than she admits.
"You coming?" she hollers at me
and I race to the ladder
and scramble up.
Mike trots back across the bridge
to meet me.

Mom and Dad stroll across the park
Dad carrying a cardboard tray
of cold drinks.
Sloane hops down
but I linger
because this moment
feels large.
This moment
feels like it needs me
to pay attention.

In this moment
with *home* in my heart
and Mike at my side
I swear
I could slay dragons.

Acknowledgments

My heartfelt thanks to all who helped bring Mike and Cara's story into being.

To the team at Pajama Press: you are extraordinary. Thank you for believing in me, and thank you especially to my editor, Ann Featherstone, for her wisdom, guidance, and support.

To the "mentors on the mountain" crew—Gabrielle Byrne, Heather Ezell, Rachel Griffin, Joy McCullough, Julia Nobel, Rebecca Schaeffer, Rebecca Sky, and Winston. You were the first to hear Mike's story. Thank you for your excellent cheerleading and your friendship.

To Kip Wilson and Carlee Karanovic, fastest beta readers ever. Thank you for your insight and enthusiasm.

To my writing tribe, especially the River Writers critique group and my PW14 Table of Trust warriors. I can't imagine doing this writing life without you.

To my dog, Mac, who models love, friendship, and loyalty every single day, and whom I may have called Mike more than once during the writing of this book. Sorry, Mac.

And to my family, near and far. I love you. You are my home, always.